MW01482782

cinnamon rolls and corpses

Snow Falls Alaska Cozy - 1

wendy meadows

Majestic Owl Publishing LLC
P.O. Box 997
Newport, NH 03773

 Created with Vellum

chapter one

Bethany Lights could hardly stand still. Excitement layered on top of fearful anticipation sounded through her heart like a million angels singing to scared children riding a frightening rollercoaster. For the first time in her life, Bethany was on her own—all alone. Usually, a courageous step out into the unknown wouldn't have been such a nerve-racking experiment, but Bethany was forty-five years old. At forty-five, a woman wanted to be settled down and secure; at least, that's what Bethany's overbearing mother had always claimed. It wasn't good for a "widow" to start over all alone, especially in Alaska.

My mother is enough to give me a migraine. Besides, she was never aware of how bad my marriage was, Bethany thought as a tall, rough-looking man in his late sixties closed a brown envelope. *That's it. The deal is closed. I now own my first cabin. Now I can get settled in and focus on the coffee shop I bought from Sarah Spencer.*

"All the papers are signed," Greg Cranmore grunted unpleasantly. "You can move into the cabin, Ms. Lights." Greg tossed a hard eye at the pretty woman standing at the end of a brown table. Bethany Lights reminded him of a red-headed Jane Wyatt. No matter. Greg didn't like new faces. New faces always brought trouble and caused him headaches. "Here's your check, Sarah Garland—"

Sarah Spencer sighed. Greg was in a very cantankerous mood. "My married name is Sarah Spencer, Greg. You know that."

"The property is still under Sarah Garland," Greg griped. He shoved the brown envelope across toward Sarah with a grumpy hand. "If you and Detective Spencer sell your cabin, I'll call you Sarah Spencer, but the coffee shop is being sold under the name Sarah Garland."

Sarah caught the envelope that slid toward her. "You're still upset because Amanda and I bought O'Mally's," she complained in a tone that told Greg to stop being so crotchety. "Don't you think it's time you stop frowning, Greg?"

"I'm upset because of the knife you put in my back," Greg snapped. He rose on a pair of painful legs, grabbed a red and green coat, and pointed a pair of hard eyes at Sarah. "You stole O'Mally's out from under me, Sarah, and you know it. You and that aggravating rodent from London."

"Amanda Hardcastle is—" Sarah fought back.

"I had a developer all lined up!" Greg slung on his coat. "You and your friend sweet-talked a dying old man into selling you his store and land. Pathetic!" Greg snapped up a pair of black gloves sitting on the table. "You're lucky I'm the only realtor in town...but the next time you want to sell something, find someone else!"

Greg stormed out of the small, warm room that held a single brown table, an old filing cabinet, and four wooden walls that still clung to the year 1971.

Sarah shook her head. "I'm sorry, Bethany. Greg Cranmore isn't the nicest man in Snow Falls. As a matter of fact, most people in Snow Falls avoid him. Unfortunately, he's the only licensed realtor in town." Sarah quickly used her left hand to brush a few pieces of dog hair off a dark green sweater before standing up. "Amanda has a new puppy," she said, trying to lighten the mood.

Bethany forced a grateful smile to her lips. Maybe Greg Cranmore was a rude man, but Sarah was definitely a tender blessing. Bethany just knew she and Sarah would be good friends. "I grew up in a house full of shedding dogs. My daddy, rest his soul, brought home every stray dog that crossed his path."

"I have a friend who does the same thing," Sarah laughed a little. "When you meet Amanda, you'll see what I'm talking about. In the meantime, I'm sure you have lots to do." She stared at the lovely woman wearing a brown dress that was noticeably new. Bethany was trying too hard to dress like a "Snow Fallian," as Sarah often called the people who lived in Snow Falls.

"The movers should be arriving around lunch time," Bethany smiled, allowing excitement and happiness to return to her heart. "I have about two hours. I think I'll go explore my new coffee shop in the meanwhile."

Sarah smiled again—but in the mind of the homicide detective she had once been, Sarah wondered why a widow appeared so happy. The urge to pry into Bethany's life scratched Sarah on the shoulder. "Amanda is babysitting Little Sarah. I have a little time. Want some company?"

"That would be great." Bethany glanced down at the wooden table, where two sets of keys were sitting at the end of the table. *Those keys represent my new life. My home...my coffee shop. I'm officially concreted in. Snow Falls is now my home.* "I suppose I am nervous," she confessed. "My entire family thinks I'm insane for moving to Alaska alone. After my husband died, my family expected me to move back to North Carolina. I was living in Tennessee at the time of his death."

"I did notice a little southern accent." Sarah watched as Bethany continued to stare down at the table. She understood how Bethany was feeling. Happy. Excited. Scared. A flood of overwhelming emotions.

"You can't take North Carolina out of a woman," Bethany told Sarah, unable to take her eyes off the keys she was staring at. *Ken was such a cruel man. For twenty-one years of my life, that man mentally and emotionally abused me. Now that's he's dead, I'm free of that awful monster. Now I can start all over. Now I can have a home of my own. Now I can finally live...in a new state, a new town...in the snow. Oh, I have always loved the snow so much.*

"Uh, Bethany...are you all right?" Sarah asked as gentle tears fell from Bethany's eyes.

"What?" Bethany asked, confused.

"You're crying."

"Am I? Oh my..." Bethany quickly raised her head. She wiped at her eyes with a gentle, soft hand. "I guess I got lost in memory lane for a second."

"Want to talk about it?" Sarah asked gingerly.

Bethany felt a fresh tear leave her eye. "You're wondering why a widow moved to your cozy little town, right? You're wondering why I seem so happy and excited when I should be sad and upset, right?"

"How bad was your marriage?" Sarah patted a brown-cushioned chair. "Please, sit down."

Bethany stared into a set of warm, loving eyes that melted her heart. Sarah Spencer was sincere inside and out. There was nothing fake about her.

"I need to stand," she told Sarah as another tear slipped from her eye. Sarah waited patiently. "For twenty-one years, Ken Branson dedicated his life to abusing me. Mentally and emotionally, never physically. Sometimes I wish he would have hit me with his hand instead of his words."

Sarah felt anger grip her heart. She knew monsters like Ken Branson all too well. "I'm sorry."

"So was I," Bethany confessed as a hard, icy wind howled outside. She turned away from the table, walked over to a small window covered by a brown curtain, and stopped. "Everyone thought I had the perfect marriage. I had to pretend." Bethany eased the curtain back with a trembling hand. A soft snow was falling outside—beautiful snow, a clean snow that had no memory of her life. "Ken was a heart surgeon. My family adored him. I had to pretend...it's complicated."

"I'm a good listener." Sarah approached Bethany, peeked outside at the snow, and waited.

Bethany stood silent for a few seconds, struggling to hold onto hope and the joy of beginning a new life. Sadness and bitterness were slowly washing up on the shores of a broken heart. "My family is very wealthy, Sarah. My daddy, rest his soul, owned a chain of toy stores throughout the southeast region of the lower states. My mother's family were all lawyers—rich lawyers." Bethany kept her eyes on the fresh, pure snow blanketing Snow Falls. "In the South, a woman is raised to be a certain way...a certain type of wife. You didn't throw light on your problems...especially your marital problems. No—a woman simply swept her problems under the rug and put on a brave face to keep her family name safe and respected."

Sarah heard a deep bitterness leave Bethany's heart. "I grew up in Los Angeles. I suppose we grew up in two different worlds."

"Not really," Bethany objected. "It doesn't matter where a woman lives. Abuse is abuse. The monsters carrying out the abuse are all the same."

"Yes, that's true."

Bethany forced her eyes away from the snow. She turned and focused on Sarah's caring eyes. "My husband had a one-million-dollar life insurance policy. He put me down as the benefactor, but...but he was planning to divorce me and marry the woman he began...well...there's no point in going into detail."

"I understand."

Bethany felt more tears slip from her eyes as one wave of bitterness after another tore down a wall of hope. "My husband didn't expect to die. He was hit by a drunk driver. Both he and the woman he was planning to marry were killed...and I...Sarah, I was left everything. It wasn't meant to be that way. Absolutely not." Bethany wiped at her tears. "I was meant to be given walking papers that included a five-thousand-dollar lifetime monthly allowance and a lousy BMW that leaked oil. But before my husband could get all his ducks in a row, he was killed. I learned this from my husband's attorney. Many ugly secrets were revealed."

"I can't imagine how hurt you felt."

Bethany heard a sour laugh leave her mouth. "My husband—my dead husband—would have removed me as his benefactor the day he was killed. As a matter of fact, Sarah —and you may not believe this—but he was actually driving to his attorney's office when a twenty-two-year-old drunk college student ended his life. Can you believe that?"

Sarah watched as more tears slipped from Bethany's eyes. *Bless her heart*, Sarah thought. Bethany was a hurt and broken woman. "Seems like maybe God had different plans?"

"I've considered that," Bethany nodded. "As horrible as the last twenty-one years were, I have always known that God was with me." Bethany turned back to the falling snow. "I got rid of my husband's last name. I freed myself of that horrible name. I sold a house that had become my prison, sold the stocks left to me, that lousy BMW—everything—and moved to Alaska."

"Why Alaska?" Sarah carefully inquired.

Bethany continued to stare at the snow. "I love the snow, Sarah, and that's the truth. When I was a little girl, I would dream of living in the North Pole where it snowed all the time. I dreamed of living on an arctic island filled with Christmas trees, toys, talking reindeer..." Bethany closed her soft eyes and allowed her heart to travel to a faraway land. "When I was sixteen, I traveled to Alaska with my daddy, rest his soul. Daddy's brother had been killed in a hunting accident and he was determined to be with the body instead of allowing the body to be flown back to North Carolina like a piece of luggage. Daddy had such a kind heart. Sometimes, deep down, I think he knew how bad my marriage was."

"I'm sure he did."

Bethany nodded. "Daddy and I were close, but sadly, my mother dominated him. Anyway, Sarah, Daddy and I stopped right here in this little town. Right here in Snow Falls...this is where the authorities brought the body. Thirty-two years ago, there wasn't much to Snow Falls—"

"There still isn't much to Snow Falls now," Sarah said, trying to make Bethany smile a little.

"Enough to call home." Bethany's eyes slowly opened. "When my husband was killed, I knew I couldn't move back home, but where could I go? I visited my daddy's grave, rest his soul, and began talking to him. And Sarah, on a cold, rainy day while I was talking to Daddy, I remember the trip I took with him to Snow Falls. As sad as the trip had been for Daddy, for me, the trip was the greatest memory I have of my daddy. Daddy and I had a wonderful time together, as strange as that might sound."

"Not strange at all."

Bethany let out a deep breath. "Daddy's brother was a hard man. Daddy wasn't very close to him, but Daddy was the type of man who carried out family obligations. That's the way it is in the South." Bethany's tears began to dry up. "I remember sitting in a little building right out there on the main street and sharing a coffee with Daddy. We got caught in a snowstorm and couldn't leave town for a week—oh, what a wonderful week that was." Bethany forced a smile to her eyes. "I wanted to return to the happiest time of my life, Sarah…and so here I am."

Sarah reached out and offered a warm hug. "You're not going to be alone, Bethany," she promised. "You have a friend now."

Bethany hugged Sarah back. "I know, and thank you." Bethany slowly let go of Sarah. "Want to know a little secret? Well, more like a miracle?"

"Sure."

"Your coffee shop...that's the same building where Daddy and I shared a cup of coffee," Bethany confessed. "When I arrived in town and saw your coffee shop was up for sale, I knew Daddy was with me. I knew my heart had led me home." Bethany fought back a few tears—happy tears—as the waves of bitterness crashing down into her heart were quickly dragged back out to sea by tender memories. "Well, there's my life story. I hope you don't think I'm insane."

"I think you're great," Sarah smiled. "If I told you my life story, I think you would have me locked away in a mental home."

"Actually, I'm aware of your life story. You're quite famous in Snow Falls, you know." Bethany patted Sarah's arm. "Let's grab our coats and talk more at the coffee shop," she stated in a voice that slowly began to fill with excitement and hope again. *Ken is dead. Why should I let that awful monster destroy my joy? Besides, I know Daddy is with me. I know I was meant to return to Snow Falls. No more tears. No more bitterness. I'm determined to put the past into a deep hole and grab a handful of fresh snow...healing, beautiful snow.*

Sarah examined Bethany's eyes. She expected there was more to the woman—far more than what appeared on the surface. Time, Sarah knew, would open up more chapters. But for the time being, Sarah was happy knowing that Bethany Lights was going to become a new member of her family.

"Well, here we are," Bethany spoke in a low but happy whisper as she stepped through a thick wooden door. The smell of forgotten coffee struck her nose like the words of a sleepy poet suddenly rising up from a closed, dusty book.

"It's a bit dusty," Sarah apologized, stepping into her old coffee shop covered with snow. Warm, inviting heat immediately greeted her frozen face. "I haven't been inside this coffee shop for over a year. Amanda and I have been very busy, and Little Sarah keeps me very busy as well."

"I can imagine," Bethany smiled as Sarah found a light switch. A sea of soft yellow light shone from a wooden ceiling and brought life to a room straight out of 1947. Bethany adored the atmosphere of the room.

"Dust or no dust, this little coffee shop is my new home," she said, beaming, then hurried to a long front counter that sung happy, nostalgic songs into the dusty air. "Oh, Sarah, this is my new life. I'm so happy...so grateful," she gushed, setting down a green purse.

A warm coffee shop is better than a creepy snowman wearing a leather jacket, Sarah thought as she watched Bethany place a loving hand onto the front counter. "Well, I don't mean to be a rock in your shoe, but remember, Bethany, this is Snow Falls. Don't expect a lot of business. I only opened the coffee shop two or three days a week. When the hard snows arrive, most people stay home or go to the local diner up the street."

"Oh, I'm not interested in money," Bethany assured Sarah. "My financial situation is secure." She turned to face Sarah, wearing a bright smile. "I have always been the type of woman who could make a penny stretch into a mile. I've never been very materialistic, either. I've always been happy with the little things in life. Buying your coffee shop was the first major gift I've ever given myself...and probably the last." A warm, though somewhat nervous happiness glowed in

Bethany's eyes, and she looked around the front room. "I bought this coffee shop because I believe God brought me to Snow Falls. I'm not in business to get rich. I'm in business to...find peace."

"And you will find peace," Sarah promised in a gentle voice. She approached Bethany and touched the woman's arm with a kind hand. "I've already showed you around the coffee shop a few days ago, so you know where everything is. I think you need to have some alone time, but I do want to see you tonight for dinner at my cabin. Please."

Bethany smiled. "I would like that very much, Sarah. Thank you."

Sarah smiled back. "My husband is out of town right now. Tonight will be an all-girls night—you, me, Little Sarah, and Amanda...and Mittens. Mittens is my Siberian Husky. She's very friendly." Sarah glanced around the front room. "Lots of memories in this room," she told Bethany, and smiled again. "Do you still have my address?"

Bethany nodded. "I have it written down and stored in my purse."

"Then I will see you tonight at six o'clock. The pizza and chocolate brownies will be waiting." Sarah offered a tender hug. "Sometimes the past can be a very painful enemy to defeat. I learned that whenever I tried to fight the past alone, I failed. I had to allow myself to be loved...and to love back. I also learned that there was no shame in crying my eyes out."

"Thank you, Sarah." Bethany hugged her new friend with grateful arms. "I think that I just might take your advice to heart."

"See you at six." Sarah checked the time and walked back to the front door. "I'll be at O'Mally's if you need me. An order of kosher hotdogs was due to arrive this morning. I need to go make sure Amanda didn't eat all the hotdogs...and hamburgers...and pretzels...and French fries." Sarah rolled her eyes. "My dear friend can clear out a buffet in ten seconds and not gain a pound. Remind me to hate her later."

Bethany laughed. "I will. Bye."

Sarah waved goodbye. "There's a little treat for you in the refrigerator," she called out, and then escaped into a white wonderland of falling snow, leaving Bethany alone in the coffee shop.

"Well, here I am. All alone in my coffee shop. My very own coffee shop." Bethany drew in a nervous breath, scanned the front room with happy eyes, and then decided to explore the back kitchen area. She located a light switch behind the kitchen door. "My, it is dusty," she admitted, allowing her eyes to stroll around a kitchen that more or less resembled the year 1964. Bethany spotted an old Westinghouse stove and refrigerator sitting against the north wall. Both appliances were still in good shape. Sarah had sold Bethany the coffee shop "As Is," which meant she left every single piece of furnishing and appliance behind for the new owner. Bethany knew Sarah was being kind—so very kind—to a scared woman who was beginning a new life in a strange, snowy land. Sarah could have left the coffee shop bare. Instead, she had left a warm life lingering behind to welcome a scared woman with healing hands.

"If dust is all I have to worry about, then I have nothing to worry about," Bethany said to herself.

Bethany slowly made her way to a broom closet that Sarah had managed to turn into a small office. The office was very cramped, but Bethany didn't mind. What was good enough for Sarah was good enough for her. "Well..." Bethany said to herself as she looked into the cramped office. A strange sound coming from the kitchen caused to her to spin around. "Oh! Well, where in the world did you come from?"

A curious—and very mischievous—raccoon was standing in the middle of the kitchen floor on his back legs while holding his front paws up into the air as if he were asking for bread.

Bethany stared at the raccoon for a few seconds, and then laughed. "Looks like I'm not alone after all." With those words spoken, she hurried to the refrigerator. "Sarah said there is a treat for me in the refrigerator...let's see." Bethany smiled when she spotted a brown plate holding a single cinnamon bun. "How nice."

The raccoon dropped down on all fours and scurried over to Bethany. Before she could move, the raccoon reached out its front paws and began pulling on the bottom of her dress.

"Alright, alright. Here, you can have half." Bethany retrieved the gift Sarah had left for her. She tore the cinnamon bun in half with a quick hand. "Here...eat before you rip my dress," she laughed, dropping half of the cinnamon bun onto the floor.

The raccoon quickly took his half and began pigging out. Bethany smiled, whispered a prayer of thanks, and began nibbling on her half of the cinnamon bun. "My, this cinnamon bun is very delicious and—"

"Anyone here?" a fussy voice called out from the front room.

"Mr. Cranmore?" Bethany hurried back into the front room. She spotted Greg standing just inside the front door shaking snow off his coat. "Oh, hello, Mr. Cranmore. I...I'm not open for business yet."

Greg eyed Bethany. "Are you alone?"

Bethany felt her stomach tighten. "For now, yes. I'm due to have dinner with Sarah Spencer at six o'clock."

"Sarah Spencer is a nuisance. That woman has brought nothing but trouble to Snow Falls," Greg barked as he slammed the front door closed. "Sarah and her friend from London are both a nuisance."

Bethany remained behind the front counter. The phone inside the coffee shop had been turned off. Bethany eyed her green purse sitting on the front counter. Her cell phone was asleep inside the purse, and a Glock 17 was also asleep inside the purse. Bethany wasn't a stupid woman. She understood the dangers of the world; people were monsters...deadly, vicious monsters. "Did I forget to sign anything, Mr. Cranmore?" she asked, struggling to understand the reason for Greg's sudden, unexpected visit.

"No, all the papers are signed," Greg confirmed, throwing his bitter eyes around the front room. "Never liked this coffee shop, but my distaste for this place isn't the reason I'm here. Ms. Lights," he stated, strengthening his angry voice, "I'm here because I want to warn you to stay away from Sarah Spencer and her friend Amanda Hardcastle. Both of those women are nothing but trouble. They'll smile to your face while holding a knife behind their backs."

Bethany eyed a very ugly, cruel, snarled-up face—a face that reminded her of a wounded wolf that was anxious to sink its fangs into anyone who dared step close enough. "Well...thank you for the advice, Mr. Cranmore, but I find Sarah Spencer to be a very pleasant woman."

Greg huffed. "You would," he snapped. "You women are all the same."

Bethany felt anger overtake her fear. She bravely reached for her purse and whipped out a cell phone. "Mr. Cranmore, I'm not going to stand here and allow you to insult me. Our business is complete. Now please leave my coffee shop before I call the police."

Greg eyed Bethany with hot, blazing eyes. "Do you think I'm afraid of the fleas in this town?" he asked Bethany through gritted teeth. "The cops in this miserable town are nothing but ground worms to me. Someday I will own this town!" He struck the front counter with a hard fist. "Don't get on my bad side! Do you hear me?! You'll regret the day you do!"

Bethany jumped a little and forced her mind to think. She

dropped her cell phone, and with a quick hand, retrieved the deadly gun. *I've spent countless hours at the firing range learning how to use this gun. I can fire this gun in my sleep if needed. I'm not going to let this jerk intimidate or frighten me. I'm through being bullied. I'm through being scared.*

"Get out of my coffee shop this very instant!" she hollered at Greg, aiming her gun directly at the man's chest.

Greg's eyes grew wide with shock. "How dare you—"

"Get out of my coffee shop and never return!" Bethany hollered again, staring at Greg with determined eyes. *Use your training...take a direct aim...hold your stance...speak in a loud, authoritative voice...show no fear…be prepared to shoot at any second.* "When you leave, I'm going to call the police and report this incident. Now get out!"

The look in Bethany's eyes clearly told Greg that if he made one wrong move, he was a dead man. He knew he had drastically underestimated her. Bethany, he realized, was a fighter. He had counted on using her past to intimidate her. He didn't need the new woman in town becoming buddies with Sarah Spencer. He had his own agenda, and Bethany Lights didn't need to become a thorn in his side. "You've just made yourself an enemy," he growled.

"No, *you* just made yourself an enemy," Bethany growled back, standing her ground. "I don't know who you think you are, Mr. Cranmore, but you will not intimidate or frighten me. I'm a fighter." She narrowed her eyes. "I'm also a woman who is connected to a very wealthy family filled with lawyers. I can make your life very difficult if you insist on being problematic. As a matter of fact, after I call the police, I'm going to contact my mother and tell her all about you. If anything were to happen to me, you will be the first person to get arrested. Now get out of my coffee shop."

Greg wanted to rip the gun right out of her hands, but he dared not try. Bethany was prepared to strike, that much was clear. "This town is mine. Someday you'll learn that," he snapped at Bethany, turned away from the front counter, and marched back outside into the snow, slamming the front door behind him.

Bethany carefully lowered her gun. "My goodness..." she whispered, struggling to remain calm. "What an awful man." Without wasting a second, she called the cops.

"Yes, this is Bethany Lights. I just bought the local coffee shop. I need an officer to come down to the coffee shop. I just had a very ugly encounter with Greg Cranmore. I was forced to pull my gun out...no, no one was hurt...Mr. Cranmore has left my coffee shop. I need to file a report, please...okay...thank you." Bethany put her cell phone down and looked at the front door with worried eyes. *I wish I could say this incident is over, but my heart is telling me this is the beginning of something very, very ugly.*

Outside in the snow, Greg Cranmore marched down a frozen sidewalk, making his way back to a stale office. As soon as he entered his office, bypassing the meeting room where Bethany and Sarah had sat earlier, a deadly voice rang out.

"Hello, Greg. How was your walk?"

"What?" Greg turned around and faced the door leading into the meeting room just in time to see a shadowy figure appear. "What are you doing here?" he demanded in a startled, angry voice. "I told you to never come here!"

"You don't have to worry about bossing me around anymore, Greg," the voice hissed.

Greg watched with terrified eyes as the shadowy figure raised a hungry gun up into the air. A silencer was attached to the barrel of the gun. "I no longer need your services, Greg. Our contract is...finished."

"Wait...don't...we had a plan...we had a plan...wait...don't..." Greg threw his hands up into the air and tried to run for his office. As soon as he spun around, four hot bullets tore into his back. Greg's body crashed forward like a clumsy rag doll, crashing halfway into his office.

"Don't worry, Greg. I'm going to carry out our plan. In time, Snow Falls will be all mine. But first I have to get rid of one more person," the shadow spoke in a hideous voice. "Ms. Bethany Lights is going to be a very useful tool."

With those words, the shadowy figure put his gun away and went to work dragging Greg Cranmore's dead body into his office. The figure escaped through a back door without being seen by anyone.

"Yes, Ms. Bethany Lights is going to be a very useful tool. By the time I'm finished with her, she's going to be thrown into a prison cell for life...or perhaps I'll just kill her off? Only time will tell."

chapter two

ethany felt her stomach tighten when the door to her new coffee shop opened. A tall red-headed man sporting a hunting beard stepped through the door. He wore a heavy brown coat and a "Chief of Police" hat that more or less resembled a cowboy hat.

Bethany always made it a habit to steer clear of cops. Why? Because there were numerous bad apples in the barrel, and it was difficult to tell who was a good cop and who was a bad cop. *Hopefully,* Bethany thought as she watched Andrew, Sarah's good friend, close the front door, *the cops in Snow Falls are all good apples.*

Andrew turned to face Bethany. He spotted a lovely woman with a worried face standing behind the warm front counter.

"Ms. Lights?"

Bethany nodded.

"My name is Andrew. I'm the chief of police," Andrew introduced himself. "Don't let the title intimidate you. I spend most of my time being fussed at by my wife or trying to figure out how to go ice fishing without getting in trouble."

Andrew's welcoming demeanor put Bethany at ease.

"Thank you for coming," she told Andrew. "I had a very ugly encounter with—"

"Greg Cranmore," Andrew cut her off in a tired voice. "Mr. Cranmore has made a very bad name for himself in Snow Falls. I don't think there is one good person in town who has anything nice to say about that man." He approached the front counter. "What happened?"

Bethany calmly explained how Greg had entered her coffee shop, bad-mouthed Sarah and Amanda, and then threatened her. "I became very frightened. I pulled my gun out of my purse and forced him to leave my coffee shop." Bethany opened her purse and carefully presented her Glock 19 to Andrew. "I have my license to carry concealed. Alaska honors my license from Tennessee. Eventually, I'll need to get my license changed over."

"There's no rush," Andrew spoke, surprising Bethany. Most cops tried to play tough, but he fully supported Bethany's right to carry a gun.

Noticing her baffled expression, he said, "Ma'am, this is Snow Falls, Alaska. Up here, the only law is a man and his gun. Sure, I wear a badge, but there's only so much I can do. As of right now, I have three part-time cops working for me and two full-time cops. I have one full-time detective. That's a total of seven men who are responsible for a county the size of a giant iceberg. It's vital that a person owns a gun or rifle this far up and be able to defend himself...or herself, in your case. There're wild animals—and wild killers—that are never far away. I don't mean to scare you by saying that, but this little town has seen its share of horror stories."

"Thank you for being so supportive," Bethany replied, feeling relief course through her heart. *Looks like this man isn't a rotten apple. As a matter of fact, it seems like this man is a good cop who actually cares.* "What will you do about Mr. Cranmore?"

"Go over to his office and have a talk with him," Andrew explained in a calm voice that put Bethany at ease. "I'll warn him to steer clear of you or face the chance of getting arrested. I'm also going to speak to the city council members and see if they can revoke the man's license. The sooner we can get Greg Cranmore out of Snow Falls, the better. He's only here to destroy the land anyway. People in Snow Falls like the land just the way it is."

"The land is very beautiful. I just bought a cabin on Candy Dream Lane."

"Yeah, Sarah told me you bought Old Man Fennigan's cabin," Andrew nodded. "You got yourself a nice cabin." He smiled a little. "I can still remember Old Man Fennigan building his cabin. He wasn't old at the time—I was about sixteen. I helped cut down a few trees...well, that was a while ago."

Bethany saw a melancholic expression touch Andrew's eyes. "Is there anything the matter?"

Andrew glanced around the coffee shop. "I used to come in here and have coffee all the time. Guess I'll start the old habit up again when you open up for business," he spoke in a low voice. "Times sure change, even here in Snow Falls. Used to be that Sarah owned this coffee shop. Now she and Amanda own O'Mally's. Used to be I knew all the faces in town, but most of the old-timers are dying off and some new faces are showing up. Sometimes I feel like I'm losing my town."

Bethany assumed she understood how Andrew felt. Or did she? Andrew was struggling to hold onto his home and Bethany was struggling to make a new home. She was a new face in town that represented change. "You said you were married?"

"Huh?" Andrew glanced back at Bethany. "Oh sure, been married for twenty-five years now. I have a son who is nineteen. He just joined the Navy. Left two weeks ago..."

Andrew sighed. "Two weeks...seems like yesterday I was teaching my boy to shoot a rifle for the first time."

"I can't imagine how hard it must be to let go."

Andrew sighed again. "Toughest thing in the world," he said, and then hurried to check the time. "Well, I better go have a talk with Mr. Cranmore. If there is anything else you need, give me a shout and—" Andrew tapped the wooden counter, "—always keep your gun close, Ms. Lights. As I said, this is Snow Falls, Alaska. Up here the law is stretched very thin, and folks know that."

"I'll keep my gun close," Bethany promised.

Andrew nodded, offered a kind smile, and then worked his way out of the coffee shop on legs that didn't seem in any hurry. He was suffering from Empty Nest Syndrome worse than his wife was.

"I'll keep my gun close," Bethany whispered as soon as Andrew closed the front door. She slid her gun under the front counter with a quick hand. As she did, her cell phone rang.

"Oh, mother..." Bethany let out a painful moan and reluctantly answered the call. "Hello, mother."

"Don't 'hello mother' me," Rebecca Lights said impatiently. "You were supposed to have called me yesterday. Did you? No." Rebecca paced around a fancy sitting room filled with priceless furniture that had been built in the early 1900s. "Is it impossible to call your mother, Bethany?"

"I forgot," Bethany confessed. "I'm sorry."

"You forgot? Bethany, are you a grown woman or a small child?" Rebecca scolded her daughter and huffed. "You're driving me into an early grave. Your father would not be pleased."

Bethany sighed. "Mother, you're seventy years old. Daddy was seventy-five when he died of cancer. That was three years ago—"

"I'm fully aware of the time Jesus took your father home to heaven, Bethany."

Bethany felt the urge to hang up, but caught her hand just in time. "Mother—"

"Don't 'mother' me!" Rebecca snapped. "First, you insisted on moving to Alaska, and then you refuse to call me. What did I ever do to you to make you hate me, Bethany?"

"Mother, I'm not going to do the same dance with you over and over. You know I love you. Moving to Alaska was a personal choice I still believe will bring peace and happiness to my life. As far as calling you, I simply forgot. I was very exhausted yesterday and fell right to sleep after dinner. That's the truth. Accept the truth or not, that's your choice."

Rebecca grew silent for a few seconds. "Are you alright?" she finally asked, simmering down her harsh tone. "Do you need anything?"

"No. I closed on my cabin and the coffee shop today," Bethany explained. "It would be nice...if you would visit me." *I must be insane to offer an open invitation. But the woman is my mother, and as much as she drives me crazy, I do love her.*

"Perhaps in time. Right now, we're two weeks away from Thanksgiving. You know how hectic it is for me this time of year. I was hoping you might fly home and attend the family gathering?"

"You know I will," Bethany promised. "If the weather permits, that is. Right now, it's snowing outside, and earlier this morning, Sarah told me this area of Alaska gets struck by powerful snowstorms. I have to drive to Anchorage to fly out, and Anchorage is very far away."

"Yes, I know," Rebecca said, letting out a miserable groan. "You're living with the grizzly bears, Bethany. You could be living next door to me in a very nice home. The choices you make..." Rebecca shook her head. "Well, the ladies from the garden club are due to arrive shortly. I have to get ready. Call me after dinner, and I mean it. Don't forget."

"I won't," Bethany promised. "Bye, mother."

"Bye."

Bethany put down her cell phone with a heavy hand. "Well, Daddy, here we are...back in Snow Falls, and mother is just as unhappy now as she was back then. Some things never change." With those words, she grew very silent and listened to an icy wind begin to scratch on the front door of the coffee shop. The wind slowly began to howl, sending an eerie sound seeping under the front door. It was at that moment Bethany truly realized just how far she truly was away from the world —and truly understood Andrew's words. In Snow Falls, Alaska, a person had to possess the ability to take care of himself. The law was more or less helpless against the land, the weather, the wild animals, and the deadly poison thriving within the heart of mankind. "I'm truly on my own up here..."

Bethany continued to listen to the howling winds as her eyes drifted around the front room. *I'm truly alone in Snow Falls. It's just me here. I have no family. Sure, Sarah seems nice, and I'm sure we'll become friends. But for now, it's just me...all alone. I have no one to turn to, no one to help me. After twenty-one years of living in an abusive marriage, I'm free, and I've run as far away from my old life as I possibly could. Now I have what I want and need...to be alone, to have room to breathe, to be able to heal. Snow Falls is very remote...and alone. This town is exactly what I need. Alone or not, for better or worse, Snow Falls is now my home and this coffee shop is mine...and this coffee shop needs dusting.*

Bethany nodded, put on a brave face, and decided to get to work dusting and cleaning her coffee shop. The strange little raccoon decided to keep her company while she did.

An hour passed. "Well, little guy," Bethany smiled, examining a spotless front room that no longer contained a grain of dust, "we'll take a break and hit the kitchen—"

Before Bethany could finish her sentence, the front door to the coffee shop opened. Sarah quickly stepped through the front door with Andrew following close behind, soaked with snow.

When Bethany read Sarah's expression, her heart dropped. "What's the matter?" she asked, walking out from behind the front counter. The raccoon scurried into the kitchen.

Sarah waited until Andrew closed the front door. "Bethany," she stated in a worried voice, shaking snow off her coat, "Greg Cranmore was found dead in his office...shot to death." Sarah's voice was worried, yes, but her eyes were full of relief. Bethany was alive and safe.

"What?" Bethany gasped.

"Afraid Sarah is right," Andrew confirmed. "Greg Cranmore is deader than a wolf trapped under ten feet of frozen ice." He quickly stomped snow off the brown boots he was wearing and looked around. "Ms. Lights, I just had the body sent to the hospital. Dr. Whitfield will do a quick examination for me, but the state will be the one who conducts an official autopsy. I...I'm afraid...because you were the last person to see Mr. Cranmore alive—"

"I didn't kill Greg Cranmore," Bethany blurted out, feeling like a frightened schoolgirl. "You can check my gun. My gun hasn't been fired in over a month."

"Afraid I'm going to have to check your gun," Andrew informed Bethany. "Now, before you get all upset, please don't. I know you didn't kill Mr. Cranmore, and so does Sarah. But the fact is, I have rules to follow, and the fact is, someone did kill Mr. Cranmore...and you're the new face in town."

Sarah approached Bethany. "A lot of eyes are going to fall on you, Bethany. When I first arrived in town, I was forced into a murder case, too. I was marked with all kinds of horrible names. There are still people in Snow Falls who are anxious to see me leave town."

Bethany could barely believe her ears. "But Sarah, I didn't

kill anyone. I moved to Snow Falls to begin a new life. I...this is completely insane."

"Ms. Lights," Andrew spoke up, "Sarah told me a little about your past. May I ask what you did before your husband died?"

"I spent my time writing children's books," Bethany struggled to explain. "I wrote numerous series...but I stopped writing three years ago after my daddy died, rest his soul. Why?"

"Did you write anything else other than children's books?" Andrew asked carefully.

Bethany felt her heart cry out in misery. She knew what Andrew was hinting at. "Yes. Before my daddy died, I wrote a full-length book under my own name. The book was my first...and my last."

"What was the book about?" Andrew asked.

"The...perfect murder..." Bethany closed her eyes. "I wrote about the perfect murder...but it was only a book. I was so upset with my husband. So angry."

"And the book took place in a small Alaskan town, right?" Sarah gently pressed. Bethany nodded yes. "Don't worry, honey. I'm on your side, but when Andrew found Greg Cranmore dead, he called me. I had to investigate your background. Please don't be upset with me."

"I'm not upset with you." Bethany opened her eyes and looked at Sarah. "I know who you are, Sarah. I know what kind of woman you are. Why would I be upset?" She reached out and took Sarah's hands. "Someone is framing me for murder, right? Isn't that it?"

Sarah stared into a pair of scared, confused eyes that broke her heart. "Could be," she confessed. "Could be Greg Cranmore's death isn't connected to you."

"But you're standing in this coffee shop," Bethany insisted. "Your presence tells me you think otherwise." She let go of Sarah's hands. *So much for making it back to North Carolina in time for Thanksgiving. I might be dead by then.*

An icy, cruel wind agreed with Bethany.

Amanda Hardcastle watched as Bethany sipped on a hot coffee. The poor woman looked absolutely miserable. "You look like you've just eaten your last chili dog, love," she spoke in a thick British accent that Bethany wanted to find charming, but could not. Her heart was bogged down with too much worry and fear.

"I'm very worried," Bethany admitted as she sipped on her coffee. Outside, a hard, angry wind was clawing against the back door of Sarah's cabin. The soft snow that had been falling earlier in the morning had transformed into a heavy blanket of white misery. "A man has been shot to death."

"Oh dear. Poor woman." Amanda reached across a round kitchen table and patted Bethany's hand. "Want some pizza, love? Food always makes me feel better."

Bethany looked into a kind, warm face that could comfort any fearful heart. Amanda Hardcastle, Bethany felt, was a very special woman. She understood why Sarah loved Amanda so deeply. "No, thank you."

"Mind if I eat the last slice?" Amanda asked.

"Go right ahead." Bethany watched as Amanda brushed a few pizza crumbs off the front of a dark blue sweater that was very stylish—a sweater that complimented Amanda's blond hair in a way that was somewhat old-fashioned rather than modern. After brushing away the pizza crumbs, Amanda buried her right hand into a greasy pizza box and fished out a gooey slice of cheese pizza.

"Come to mama," Amanda beamed.

"You're going to turn into a slice of pizza," a teasing voice spoke. Bethany turned her head and saw Sarah appear in the kitchen doorway.

"A dream come true, love," Amanda stated happily, then went to town devouring the slice of pizza she was holding.

Sarah rolled her eyes. Amanda was a nut. "Little Sarah is asleep. The winds always put her to sleep."

"Your daughter is very beautiful, Sarah." Bethany put down her coffee. "She looks just like you."

"Little Sarah will be two years old soon." Sarah walked over to the kitchen counter and examined a baby monitor. "Little Sarah was born with a condition that makes her appear like she's not aging. She'll need constant care for the rest of her life."

"Oh Sarah, I'm so sorry." Bethany felt her heart break for Sarah.

"Thank you, Bethany, but the truth is, other than Little Sarah's condition, Dr. Rains has assured me that she's very healthy. As a matter of fact, Dr. Rains told me that Little Sarah will probably live well into her eighties or even her nineties." Sarah made sure the baby monitor sitting on the kitchen counter was in good working order and went to fetch herself a cup of coffee. "Little Sarah will need constant care because her body will never outgrow the body of a child, and neither will her mind. According to Dr. Rains, at best, we can expect Little Sarah to reach the mental ability of a third grader."

"That just makes a very special little angel more special, love," Amanda smiled as pizza sauce dripped from her lip. "Little Sarah may remain a runt for life, but she's our runt...and our angel."

Sarah smiled at Amanda. "I think you got pizza sauce on your sweater."

"Leftovers for later, love," Amanda teased.

Sarah laughed. "I bet," she said, pouring herself a cup of hot coffee. "Bethany, you don't have to feel upset or sad over Little Sarah's condition. My daughter may be small, but she carries all the love of a giant warrior inside her heart." Sarah walked over to the kitchen table and sat down. "I know this might sound selfish, but I'm glad Little Sarah will need my care the rest of her life. That means she will never leave home. I'll always have my baby."

Bethany admired Sarah's attitude—and heart. "I've never had children. I can't offer an honest opinion on what it would be like to raise a child and have that child leave home. I suppose your position is...oh, listen to me, I sound like a lawyer. I'm sorry." Bethany rubbed her tired eyes. "Sarah, I can understand why you wouldn't want Little Sarah to leave home. Little Sarah is a very precious gift."

Sarah reached out and touched Bethany's arm. "Still upset, I see. It's alright if you are."

"I don't mean to be upset, but I can't stop thinking about Mr. Cranmore. Yes, the man was hostile and rude, but murder..." Bethany shook her head. "Sarah, I consider myself to be an educated woman. Practical, self-reliant, capable of thinking on my feet when needed. I don't consider myself a foolish woman who caves into fear or fright. But right now, I have to admit my emotions are on a rollercoaster ride."

"I bet, love," Amanda declared, polishing off the last of her pizza. "First, you have to deal with a sleazy husband who was planning to ditch you for some dime-store mannequin, and then you get stuck with a dead stiff right here in Snow Falls. If I were in your shoes, I would be buying tons of hair dye to hide tons of gray hair."

"It's alright to be upset," Sarah confirmed again in a caring voice. "I'm upset myself. Mr. Cranmore was shot in the back four times. That tells me he tried to run before he was shot."

"Yes, I've considered that, too," Bethany admitted. "I've been thinking about what you told me, Sarah. Mr. Cranmore was shot dead in his office building. You found no signs of forced entry—the front and back door were both locked, which might mean the shooter had keys to the building...which implies that the shooter possibly knew Mr. Cranmore."

"Look at you!" Amanda clapped her hands. "Why, love, you're a regular Nancy Drew."

Bethany felt her cheeks turn red. "No, Amanda. I've read countless murder mystery books in my life. I have every episode of *Murder, She Wrote* and *Columbo* memorized. I'm also a fan of Nancy Drew, the Hardy Boys, and Dick Tracy. When you're trapped at home all the time with nothing to do, you find ways to entertain yourself."

"I would have baked cookies," Amanda joked in a way that made Bethany laugh.

"I tried to bake cookies, but there's only so many cookies a woman can eat," Bethany laughed. "Besides, my daddy, rest his soul, loved murder mysteries. Daddy and I swapped books, watched movies and television shows together...when he had the time, that is. I...well, all I can say is that whenever Daddy and I watched an episode of *Columbo* together, it was very special."

"I bet it was," Sarah smiled. "I can tell you miss your daddy very much."

"Oh, I do. Daddy was my very best friend. My only friend, it seemed." Sadness dripped into Bethany's voice. "Daddy was my everything. I know he's with Jesus now in glory...and someday we'll be together. Daddy always told me that death isn't the end. Death is just a quick wave goodbye until the other person catches up to the departing train and gets on. The people left behind are just lingering on a thin thread until it's time for them to use their train tickets. We're all going to die someday. Daddy was just closer to the front of the line, that's all."

"I had a dream last year," Amanda spoke up in her thick British accent. "I dreamed I saw Jesus our Lord standing on a white cloud waving at me. Jesus wasn't calling me to come to Him...He was just waving at me in a way that put my heart at ease. Then I woke up." Amanda smiled. "When I was much younger—I'll never reveal my age—"

"Forty-something," Sarah teased.

Amanda tossed a warning expression at Sarah. "There's a lot of snow outside, love. Don't make me turn you into a snowman."

"Just as long as you don't turn my nose into a carrot," Sarah pleaded.

"Oh, do you have any carrots?" Amanda asked in a hopeful voice. "And maybe some cream cheese?"

"You're the only woman I know who dips a carrot in cream cheese." Sarah rolled her eyes. "Tell Bethany about what happened to you when you were nineteen."

"Oh, well," Amanda rubbed her hands together. "When I was nineteen, I became very ill. I was put in the hospital for two straight weeks. At one point, I was told that I actually died. During that time, I think I visited heaven. I remember waking up in a beautiful place that was glowing with so many bright colors that aren't here on earth. I heard angels singing...children laughing...and in the distance, I saw a glowing golden city that I wasn't allowed to visit. Oh, love, it was so peaceful. I felt so much love...a love that consumed every fiber of my soul. I knew I was home and never wanted to leave. But this angel...he told me I had to go back because it wasn't my time. I argued with the angel, but I didn't win the argument. In heaven, the angels always win." Amanda sighed. "So anyway, here I am. And when it's my time to get on the train, as you and your daddy say, I won't be scared. No way. I'll be running as fast as I can to the train."

Bethany felt a strange peace touch her worried heart. "That's a very beautiful testimony, Amanda. Thank you for sharing. I'll treasure your words for life."

Amanda reached out and touched Bethany's arm. "Love, for those who belong to Jesus, the unimaginable awaits us. But for now," Amanda drew in a deep breath, "we're stuck here on planet earth in the flesh, which means we have to live and breathe and eat and poop. It also means we have to deal with some very ugly monsters."

"Yes, we do," Bethany sighed. She looked at Sarah. "You don't have any leads, do you?"

"No, afraid not," Sarah confessed in a miserable voice. "The back alley was snowed over by the time Andrew found Mr. Cranmore's body. Andrew found Mr. Cranmore's office locked but spotted the man's truck parked outside. Andrew assumed Mr. Cranmore was in town. He checked the diner and took a quick look around, but came up empty-handed. Andrew walked back to Mr. Cranmore's office. By this time, he was becoming suspicious, so he called a locksmith. You know the rest of the story from there, Bethany."

"All within an hour." Bethany shook her head. "It's amazing...one minute, a man was standing before me alive, and within the hour, he was shot and killed."

"Death is sudden," Sarah confirmed in a voice that sent a chill down Bethany's spine. "Right now, Andrew is checking for any new faces in town. So far, he's come up empty-handed. No one has checked into the hotel other than you. Because Thanksgiving is so close, people tend to leave Snow Falls and travel to be with family members." Sarah took a sip of her coffee and listened to the icy winds scratching at the back door. "Could it be, Bethany, that the killer left Snow Falls? Could be that Mr. Cranmore had some enemies no one was aware of? If that's the case...then so be it."

"Do you believe that's the case?" Bethany asked Sarah in a voice tinged with hope instead of despair.

"I'm wondering..." Sarah put down a brown coffee cup. "Bethany, if you were the target, why didn't the killer strike while Mr. Cranmore was inside the coffee shop—your coffee shop?" Sarah pointed out. "It seems to me that the killer was waiting for Mr. Cranmore to return to his office."

"It does seem that way..." Bethany rubbed her eyes.

"Sarah, you told me nothing was missing from Mr. Cranmore's office. No files...nothing. You also told me Mr. Cranmore's cabin wasn't disturbed. It would seem that whoever shot Mr. Cranmore did their job and left Snow Falls without being seen, but something in your eyes tells me you're still worried."

"Route 16," Sarah confessed. "Route 16 is a very long stretch of lonely road that the state patrol barely touches. We're talking about over fifty miles of bare road that is rarely patrolled. The closet town is Ice Ridge, which ends at the end of Route 16. Anyone can escape from Snow Falls when Route 16 is passable...and anyone can return."

"Return?" Bethany asked, feeling the hair on the back of her neck stand up.

"Return, love?" Amanda gulped.

"Call me irrational, but I keep having a horrible feeling that whoever killed Mr. Cranmore has left Snow Falls for now, but might return. Why? I'm not sure yet. I'm hoping and praying I'm wrong." Sarah glanced at the back door. "Time will tell. In the meantime, there's nothing we can do except get you settled in, Bethany. The snow is supposed to let up after midnight. Tomorrow, the plows will clear the roads. Amanda and I will help you get settled into your cabin. I'm just thankful your cabin is right down the road from Amanda."

"Neighbors," Amanda told Bethany, forcing a smile to her eyes. "Don't worry, love. Los Angeles and I—Los Angeles is a nickname I have for Sarah—we've been through a lot of murder cases. Why, one time, we faced a killer who infected us with a virus. We still have to go get our blood tested once every six months, and what about that horrible game show you were on, love?" Amanda asked Sarah.

"Don't remind me," Sarah moaned.

Amanda folded her arms. "When Sarah first arrived in Snow Falls, she was greeted by a creepy snowman wearing a leather jacket and chewing a candy cane." Amanda shook her head. "Love," she told Bethany, "Los Angeles and I have fought countless ugly monsters. We're used to the nightmares."

"What Amanda is trying to say is, you are not alone, Bethany," Sarah promised a very upset and worried woman. "Now, there's nothing else we can do until Andrew calls, so why don't we play Scrabble and afterward we'll bake a cake?"

"Chocolate cake, and I get the first slice!" Amanda exclaimed. "And I get to go first at Scrabble." She turned to Bethany. "I always make the best words."

"You always cheat," Sarah coughed under her breath, and then hurried out of the kitchen.

"I don't cheat and you know it!" Amanda cried, then let out a sweet giggle. "Well, maybe when I play Conrad. But he's a bloke who can't spell the word 'cat.'"

Bethany tried to smile, but her mind walked back to a very ugly morning. Somewhere out in the snow, a killer was waiting.

Far away, the deadly killer Bethany feared checked the time. "I'll make Anchorage in good time. When Thanksgiving is over, after I've given everyone time to calm down, I'll return to Snow Falls. Ms. Bethany Lights better enjoy her Thanksgiving turkey because it's going to be her last." The killer grinned. "Enjoy your turkey, Ms. Lights. Enjoy your turkey."

chapter three

Thanksgiving arrived quickly and left Snow Falls without incident, leaving Bethany feeling uneasy and confused. Greg Cranmore was dead. Had his killer simply vanished into the snow, never to return? Had the killing been tied to a personal agenda that had nothing to do with Bethany? For the time being, that's how the situation certainly appeared. Yet, Bethany couldn't shake the feeling that Greg Cranmore's death was somehow still casting a dark shadow over her heart.

I should have traveled home for Thanksgiving. The weather had cleared up enough for me to travel, but I couldn't risk putting my family in danger. I know mother was very upset, but mother is going to have to remain upset for now, Bethany thought as she used a warm washcloth to wipe down the front counter of her coffee shop. *At least I'm finally open for business. Today is my official first day. It's snowing outside, but not too bad. I should get one or two customers.*

"Right?" Bethany spoke to the sleepy raccoon lying behind the front counter on a brown dog bed. The raccoon simply let out a little snore. She smiled. "Right."

Bethany continued to wipe down the front counter with

nervous hands. As she did, the front door plowed open, revealing Amanda.

"Hey, love," Amanda called out, soaked with snow. "Brought you a pizza for lunch. Figure you might be sick of turkey leftovers."

A happy smile touched Bethany's lips. Amanda was becoming a close and dear friend Bethany adored and loved. "How did you know I was hungry?" she asked, watching Amanda stomp snow off a pair of white winter boots.

"A woman can always use a pizza," Amanda teased. "Sarah sends her love. She's at O'Mally's. We're having a sale on winter sweaters, even though it's not officially winter just yet. But in Snow Falls—" she grinned, "—winter is year round." She hurried to the front counter and set down a large pizza box. "Where's that rascally raccoon?"

"Asleep," Bethany smiled. She pointed a finger at her sleeping friend.

"Well, when he wakes up, give him this." Amanda fetched a handful of turkey-flavored dog treats out of the front pocket of her dark blue coat. "There's cheese in the middle."

Bethany watched Amanda set the dog treats down on the front counter. "You're spoiling that silly raccoon."

"I sure am, love." Amanda tipped Bethany a wink. "I wish my husband would spoil me. That lazy bloke is at home right now watching a hockey game and eating leftover pumpkin pie."

"Love is grand." Bethany folded her arms over a pink and white sweater. "Your husband seems like a very nice man. I enjoyed meeting him."

"That bloke is only nice when there's food around," Amanda teased, then checked the time. "Well, love, I hate to rush off, but I have to get back to O'Mally's. There's a chili dog calling my name." Amanda looked around the coffee shop. "I'll always love this coffee shop...it's a very special place to me."

Bethany sighed. "You're my first customer today and it's nearly lunch."

"You'll get some customers," Amanda promised. "It took people a while to get used to Sarah." She squeezed Bethany's hand. "Give it time."

"I will," Bethany promised. Amanda smiled and hurried back outside into a steady falling snow.

"Time is all I have right now," Bethany whispered, forcing a brave tone to her voice. "I guess I'll see what kind of pizza Amanda brought me."

Bethany opened up the greasy pizza box and spotted a gooey cheese pizza. She smiled and made her way to the back kitchen to gather up a plate. When she returned to the front counter, she spotted a man standing at the front door, kicking snow off a pair of black boots.

"Oh, hello. I didn't hear the door open," she called out in a startled voice. *I'm going to have to get used to people coming inside my coffee shop. I have to stop being so jumpy. This is a business, after all. I need customers to stay afloat...even though I don't really need money.*

Brian Amerson tossed a pair of hard eyes toward Bethany. "Your sign outside said you were open," he replied in a voice that caused Bethany's stomach to tighten.

"Yes, my coffee shop is open." Bethany stared at the man. He appeared to be in his late fifties or early sixties. He looked like a rugged hunter, according to the way he was dressed. Surely the man was a local.

Brian marched up to the front counter and sat down on a brown stool. He threw his eyes at a large chalkboard menu that had a list of coffees and pastries written on it in white chalk. "Black coffee...and I'll take a cinnamon bun." He snatched off a gray muffler hat and tossed it on the front counter. "Warm my cinnamon bun up."

"Of course." Bethany glanced down to where her hidden Glock 19 was sitting within arm's reach. "Allow me to take my lunch back to the kitchen." Bethany quickly scooped up her pizza and hurried back to the kitchen. "Calm down. He's just a customer, some local. This is Alaska. Not everyone who comes into the coffee shop is going to be Jimmy Stewart and Donna Reed."

Bethany tossed her pizza onto the brown kitchen counter along with the plate she was carrying, then hurried to bring out a tray of delicious cinnamon buns Sarah and Amanda had taught her how to bake during Thanksgiving. She quickly slid the entire tray of cinnamon buns into a cold oven, turned the oven on, set a timer, and then rushed back out to the front room. "Your cinnamon bun will be ready in ten minutes," she announced. "The oven I have is cold—"

"That will be fine," Brian barked. "I'll have my coffee while I wait."

Calm down. You're as nervous as a tick on the back of a speeding semi-truck. This guy is just a customer...but if that's true, why is he in my coffee shop instead of the diner? It's near lunchtime.

Bethany turned her back to Brian, studied a lunch tray holding four coffee cups, then slid her worried eyes over to the right and examined two old-fashioned coffee machines. *Why is this guy in my coffee shop? And why did he appear right after Amanda left? Had he been watching my coffee shop?* Feeling her chest tighten, she carefully poured Brian a hot cup of black coffee. "Careful...hot," she said, setting the coffee cup down on the front counter.

Brian ignored Bethany's warning. He picked up the coffee cup and took a sip of coffee that burned his tongue. "You're new in Snow Falls," he grunted.

"Yes, I am," Bethany admitted, stepping closer to her gun. She quickly glanced down at the floor, seeing the raccoon was no longer in his bed. "Are you a local?"

"Yeah," Brian nodded, staring at Bethany with hard, brutal eyes. "Lived in Snow Falls for the past ten years. Like to keep to myself. Had to drive into town and get some supplies. Figure I'd stop and get a cup of coffee before driving back to my place."

See? He's just a local. A grumpy local, a creepy local, but just a local. Bethany struggled to calm her heartbeat. "What's your name?" she asked. "My name is Bethany Lights."

"I stay to myself," Brian grunted at her.

"Oh. Well, of course. I understand." Bethany glanced over her shoulder back toward the kitchen. *Ring, timer. The quicker this guy leaves my coffee shop, the better.* "Well, I'll go check on your cinnamon bun. Excuse me."

She hated to leave her gun behind, but Brian's hard eyes drove her back into the kitchen. "What a creepy man," she whispered in a shaky voice. "I just need to calm down and serve that man his cinnamon bun and get him out of my coffee shop."

Bethany impatiently waited for the tray of cinnamon buns sitting in the oven to warm up. When the timer went off, she quickly slapped a hot cinnamon bun down onto a green plate, added a few lines of icing across the top of the cinnamon bun, and hurried back to the front room. "Here you are. Hot and fresh."

Brian watched her set down a fresh, delicious cinnamon bun. He would eat the cinnamon bun before attacking. "Got a fork?"

"Of course." Bethany brought a fork out of a silver canister sitting on the back counter. He snatched the fork from her hand. "Well, I'll be in the kitchen if you need anything—"

"More coffee." He held up his coffee cup with his left hand. Bethany bit down on her lower lip and carried out a quick refill order.

"I'll be in the kitchen." Bethany forced a weak smile to her worried eyes and walked away, leaving Brian alone. *I'm going to call Andrew...no, that would be silly. What would I say? There's a creepy man in my coffee shop who's eating a cinnamon bun?*

She scolded herself over being so silly, yet her heart was

insisting something was horribly wrong. She had trained herself how to read the eyes of a person. Her worried heart clearly insisted that the man sitting in her coffee shop was a monster. "Okay...enough."

Bethany reached into the front pocket of a heavy dress that was resting under a warm sweater. She pulled out her cell phone and called Sarah.

Sarah picked up on the third ring. "Ladies...you're going to tear that sweater...stop fighting...Mrs. Johnson, you're eighty years old...stop fighting over that sweater with Mrs. Hamilton...Mrs. Hamilton, put your wooden cane down!"

"Sarah...Sarah, are you there?"

"Oh, hi Bethany. Sorry, it's insane this morning," Sarah spoke wearily.

"Oh, well, you do seem to have your hands full. Sorry I bothered you."

"No, honey, I always have time for my friends—Mrs. Johnson, don't you dare throw your false teeth at Mrs. Hamilton!" Sarah rolled her eyes. "Is everything okay?"

"Oh, sure. I got my first customer. Some guy who is...well...nothing." Bethany felt silly. "I guess I'm still a little jumpy. I have to get used to people coming into my coffee shop."

Sarah heard a deep concern in her friend's voice that caused her to turn away from the two old women at war over a silly sweater. "I'll call Andrew and tell him to walk down to your coffee shop."

"Oh no. It's silly, really," Bethany insisted, keeping her voice low. "I can't jump at every shadow, Sarah. It's been over three weeks since Greg Cranmore was killed. I'm sure the killer is far away." Bethany drew in a deep breath. "I know you're busy. I'll let you go."

"Are you sure?"

"I'm sure," Bethany promised. "Bye. I'll see you tonight for dinner. My place, remember?"

"Amanda and I will be ready at six," Sarah assured Bethany, then reluctantly ended the call.

"Something isn't right," Sarah said to herself. She quickly dialed Andrew's number.

"Andrew, can you take a walk down to the coffee shop? Bethany has a customer who's making her feel uneasy."

"Sure thing," Andrew said as he tossed a half-eaten cheeseburger onto his messy desk.

"I know we've only known Bethany for a short while, but I have come to realize that she's a very brilliant woman who doesn't overreact," Sarah told Andrew in a worried voice.

"Yeah, Bethany is the type of woman that benefits a town," Andrew agreed, slapping on his coat. "My wife sure likes her. Too bad Bethany is all broken inside. I sure hope she starts to heal soon."

"I was broken when I arrived in Snow Falls, too," Sarah reminded him. "Call me after you check on Bethany."

"Sure thing."

Sarah put down her cell phone and glanced around the warm, cozy department store that had become her second home. Oh, how Sarah loved O'Mally's—how she loved Snow Falls. *I fought to be here, to belong here. I have a feeling Bethany is going to have to take the same snowy path I was forced to take.* "Mrs. Johnson, stop trying to hit Mrs. Johnson with your pocketbook!"

Bethany didn't hear Sarah yelling at an ornery old lady. She carefully walked back into the front room to check on her customer. "How is your—" she began to ask, but then froze. Brian's face was planted face down over his half-eaten cinnamon roll. His hands were lying limp at his side. Hot coffee was spilled all over the front counter, dripping down onto the man's lap. A sticky fork was lying in the mess of spilled coffee.

"Oh my goodness!" Bethany cried out, stumbling back to the kitchen door. Feeling her panicked mind transfer to autopilot, she snatched her cell phone and called the police station.

"Yes, this is Bethany Lights. I need help. There's a man lying unconscious..." she struggled to explain the situation to a sleepy cop who had been munching on a plate of French fries. "What...oh, he is...okay..."

Bethany tossed her cell phone away and ran to the front door. She yanked the front door open, stuck her head out into a snow that was falling much heavier now, and spotted Andrew trailing toward the coffee shop, working his way down a frozen sidewalk. "Andrew!" she called out and began waving her arms. "Hurry!"

Andrew spotted Bethany in the snow. He threw his legs into high gear, yanked out a fierce Glock 17, and hightailed it down the sidewalk.

Bethany grabbed his arm and pulled him into the coffee shop. "There," she pointed at the front counter. "I went in the back and called Sarah. When I came back to the front room, he was crumpled over on the front counter."

"Is there anyone else here?" Andrew asked sharply.

Bethany shook her head.

He closed the front door. "Stay here, Ms. Lights," he ordered, and then cautiously approached the front counter. His eyes soaked in the scene. Without having to think twice, he knew the man slumped over on the front counter was dead. He approached the body and checked for a pulse.

"Is he dead?" Bethany asked, watching Andrew checking Brian's throat for a pulse.

Andrew nodded.

"Oh my..."

Andrew placed a call to the police station. "Henry, call

Conrad. He's at home. Today was his day off. Tell him I have a dead body at the coffee shop...yeah...I know." He glanced back at Bethany. He spotted a very scared woman. "Get an ambulance down here...have Mac plow the front streets. You and Fred need to mark off the area...yeah...thanks, Henry."

He ended the call with a weary heart. "Ms. Lights, I..." He couldn't finish his sentence. What could he say? Two men were dead, and Bethany was trapped right in the middle of a poison pit.

Outside in the snow, a deadly killer grinned and walked away.

chapter four

Conrad Spencer shook his head as two young paramedics hauled a black body bag out of Bethany's coffee shop. "There's nothing more I can do here," he spoke in a clear cop voice. "Dr. Whitfield will do a quick examination, but it's clear the victim was poisoned."

Bethany watched Conrad place his hands into the pockets of a worn-down, black leather jacket. Conrad reminded her of a tough New York street cop.

"Detective Spencer, I didn't kill that man," she insisted, standing off to the side with Sarah and Amanda.

"We'll have the cinnamon bun tested along with the others," Conrad explained, keeping his voice neutral. His gut told him that Bethany was no killer, but he barely knew the woman. Killers, he had learned from experience, were dangerously clever people; evil creatures who manipulated even the most brilliant of minds. "The cinnamon bun does seem to be the carrier."

Sarah studied Conrad's face. She knew her husband didn't believe Bethany Lights was a killer, but still...Conrad was keeping a safe distance, which meant everyone else in Snow Falls would take the same route. For the time being, Bethany was on her own.

"Honey, you're sure you didn't see anyone?" she asked Bethany.

"No," Bethany insisted. "I called you, Sarah, because that awful man was making me feel very uncomfortable. I'm sorry he's dead..." Bethany paused, rubbing her shaky hands together. "Sarah," she managed to calm her voice down, "I didn't kill that man. I don't know who did, but I fear that whoever killed Greg Cranmore is behind this...and for whatever reason, the killer has involved me. I don't know why. I could be wrong."

"Brian Amerson had been living in Snow Falls for about ten years," Andrew spoke, standing close to Conrad. "I remember when he moved to Snow Falls. I had to write him a ticket for hunting on private land. The guy was never nice to anyone. Kept to himself. I saw him only when he drove into town to get supplies. Amerson lived about twenty miles north of Snow Falls in a remote cabin. Mr. McCrandy's land borders the man's land. Caught the man hunting on Mr. McCrandy's land four times."

"Are you sure Brian Amerson was hunting?" Sarah asked Andrew.

"He had a hunting rifle with him and was dressed in hunting gear, so sure seemed that way," Andrew answered.

"Isn't Mr. McCrandy ninety-five years old?" Conrad asked.

"Ninety-five, and still as young and spry as a sixteen-year-old," Andrew stated matter-of-factly. "That old man is going to outlive us all."

Conrad looked at Sarah. "I have to check Brian Amerson's cabin and then have a talk with Mr. McCrandy. I'll be late getting home."

Sarah understood Conrad's tone. He was clearly warning her not to involve herself in the murder case. "Mrs. Fleishman is watching Little Sarah, Conrad. I can—"

"You're going home," Conrad insisted. "Amanda, take

Sarah home. Ms. Lights," he turned his attention to Bethany. "For now, I think you'll be safer at the station."

"Are you placing me under arrest?" Bethany asked, forcing her voice to not reveal her worry and fear. It was time to start thinking.

"No. But there is a killer loose, and right now you need to be watched," Conrad explained.

"Conrad is right," Andrew spoke up. "Ms. Lights, remember what I told you a few weeks ago. This is Snow Falls, where the law can only do so much. If you go back to your cabin, there's not much I can do except send a patrol out. The snow is falling mighty hard, which means your road won't be passable come nightfall. Mac stops running his plows when night arrives." He drew in a tired breath. "You'll be safer at the station where I can keep an eye on you."

"I'm afraid Andrew is right, love," Amanda told Bethany, taking the woman's hand into her own. "I'll call my hubby and tell him I'll be staying at the station tonight with you. I don't want you to be alone." Before Sarah could speak up, Amanda shook her head at her. "You need to be with Little Sarah, love. I'll stay with Bethany. Tomorrow night, you can stay with her, and I'll stay with Little Sarah."

Sarah hesitated, then agreed. *I can investigate this case more if I'm at home anyway.* "Alright," she stated in a way that put Conrad at ease. "I'll go home."

"Then let's move," Andrew ordered. "Daylight is wasting."

Andrew helped Bethany lock down the coffee shop and walked her outside into a heavy falling snow tossed around by a howling wind. "Temperature is dropping, Conrad," he called out. "Snow is getting heavier by the minute. I don't think you'll be able to reach Brian Amerson's cabin today. Roads are probably impassable up that way by now anyway."

"My truck has a plow attached to it, Andrew. I have to check the cabin and speak to Mr. McCrandy."

"As far as we know, Mr. McCrandy might be dead," Andrew hollered back over the howling winds.

"Have Henry watch Ms. Lights, Andrew. You're coming with me."

"I was afraid of that!" Andrew turned to face Bethany, Sarah, and Amanda. "Sarah, walk Ms. Lights down to the station and tell Henry to keep a sharp eye on her. Tell Fred to stay at the station, too." He turned back to Conrad. "Remind me to hate you later. Let's move!"

Conrad gave Sarah a quick kiss and hurried off with Andrew at his side.

"Please, Jesus, protect them," Sarah prayed.

"Amen," Amanda added. She reached out and locked arms with Bethany and Sarah. "Let's go before we turn into frozen snowmen."

Bethany tucked her head against the wind and began walking up a snow-scarred sidewalk, moving past old wooden buildings that were being battered by the howling winds and hard-falling snow. She walked past glowing windows that made her feel as if her heart had somehow entered the time of Ebenezer Scrooge.

*Scrooge...Scrooge...*she heard Jacob Marley's spooky voice calling out. *Scrooge...Scrooge.*

She stopped and looked directly at a glowing window that displayed freshly cooked bread, cakes, and pies. The Snow Fall Bakery was up and running, yet the bakery seemed lost and forbidden.

"I wanted to begin a new life, but instead, I've stepped into a snowy nightmare," she whispered, feeling her heart fill with a deep, sharp fear attached to hideous fangs—fangs that were hungry for her heart.

"Come on, love," Amanda called out over the wind. She got Bethany moving again and didn't stop until her legs walked into the warm police station.

A tall, skinny, gray-haired man named Henry Torks was

standing in a small front room lined with four wooden desks. "Coffee, Henry. Please tell me you have some coffee made," Amanda begged.

Henry pointed to a small coffee station that was nestled up against the north wall. "You know me, Amanda. I never go without my coffee," he spoke in a friendly voice. Henry was fifty-nine, married to a lovely Christian woman, and had two sons and three grandchildren who lived in the lower states. He was a decent man who spent his time reading his Bible and making rocking chairs when he wasn't on duty. Even when Henry was on duty, he read his Bible.

"Bless you!" Amanda hurried to the coffee station. "The wind is horrible."

Sarah glanced around. Fred Cunningham was nowhere in sight. "Henry, where is Fred?" she asked.

"At the hospital," Henry explained. "His wife called. She slipped and hurt her ankle about the same time the ambulance pulled off. I was going to tell Andrew, but if he's not here, I'm guessing Conrad decided to check Brian Amerson's cabin and talk to Old Man McCrandy." Henry shook his head. "Conrad sure is a hard-headed fella. He's given Andrew lots of gray hair."

"Conrad has given me gray hair, too," Sarah assured him. She turned her attention to Bethany. "Henry—"

"You'll be safe here," Henry promised Bethany, reading Sarah's eyes.

"Thank you, Officer Torks—"

"Call me Henry," he insisted and offered a kind smile. "And if it's alright, I'll call you Bethany. My daddy taught me it's not right to call a person anything other than his—or her —first name."

Bethany was shocked that Henry was being so nice. "Aren't you worried I might be a killer?" she asked, feeling a hint of bitterness enter her voice. "I mean, I am the new woman in town, right? Two men are dead, right? Everyone is going to think I'm the killer, right?"

"The dummies will think you're poison," Henry nodded. "Snow Falls has its share of dummies. But the folks that have some sense in their minds will see things differently." Henry nodded at Sarah. "Sarah was marked as a poisonous leaf when she arrived in Snow Falls, too. Took a while for folks to realize she was just plain jinxed."

"Thanks a lot, Henry." Sarah rolled her eyes. "I'm not that jinxed."

Henry let out a simple laugh. "Maybe, maybe not," he told Sarah, and then focused back on Bethany. "You can sleep in one of the holding cells. I'll get you a blanket—"

"Make that two blankets," Amanda called out from the coffee station. "I'm spending the night, too...and you better get me some fresh donuts. These donuts are stale!" Amanda held up a stale chocolate donut. "Really, Henry?"

"Fuss at Fred. He's the one who's in charge of the donuts," Henry defended himself.

"Lazy blokes," Amanda mumbled to herself.

Henry laughed again. "She never changes, does she?" he asked Sarah.

"No," Sarah sighed. *And I wouldn't have it any other way.* "Well, I better get home while I still can. Mrs. Fleishman still has to get home, too." Sarah turned to Bethany. "We'll get to the bottom of this, but I'm going to need your help, Bethany. I can tell that you're a brilliant woman. I read your book. You're a skilled writer. Please don't let anger and bitterness cloud your mind."

"Why not?" Bethany replied, feeling bitterness slap her fear away with a vicious baseball bat. "My husband abused me and then betrayed me. No one ever stepped up to help me or care for me. My daddy, rest his soul, knew...but what could he do?" Bethany felt her cheeks flush red with anger. "And now two men are dead. So much for a fresh new start in my winter wonderland. My winter dream, right, Sarah?"

Sarah understood how Bethany was feeling—she understood the woman's anger, fear, frustration, and desperation. Pain caused many harmful splinters to stick in a person's heart. "You have to fight, Bethany. Don't give up. There is hope."

A tear slipped from Bethany's eye. She threw up her right hand and slapped the tear away. "How many tears does a woman have to cry before she finds peace, Sarah? How many?" she demanded. "If my mother found out the truth, she would demand I move back to North Carolina at once, and if I refused, she would try to have me admitted to a mental hospital. My entire family can be very controlling. That's one of the reasons I so desperately wanted to move to Snow Falls—this was the one town I remember having peace in. When Daddy and I came here to take care of his brother's body, we had peace. Is that so horrible?" More and more tears began to fall from Bethany's eyes. "Is it so horrible to want peace, Sarah?"

Sarah stepped forward and put her arms around Bethany. "No, honey, it's not," she whispered. "You go ahead and cry it out. I'm right here."

Bethany felt her arms slowly raise up into the air. Instead of pushing Sarah away, she simply embraced the woman. "I'm scared...confused...angry...frustrated...and yes, very hurt," she confessed and then simply cried.

"Oh!" Amanda ran to Bethany and hugged her. "It's alright, love, we're here. We're—"

Before Bethany could cry another tear, the front door to the police station opened. Everyone turned just in time to see Julie Walsh appear. Amanda nearly hit the floor.

"Your hubby told me you were here," Julie spoke in a warm British accent that matched Amanda's and forced a strained smile to her lips. "Cousin Amanda, how are you?"

"Cousin Amanda?" Sarah asked in a confused voice. "Amanda, you didn't tell me—"

"Oh my..." Amanda's jaw nearly hit the floor. "It can't be...Julie...oh my..." She slowly let go of Bethany and stared at a woman who resembled a very young and beautiful Judi Dench.

Julie quickly brushed thick snow off a gray snow coat and pulled off a white snow cap, revealing lovely black hair. "Don't hate me for showing up so unexpectedly," she told Amanda in a tense voice. "I know this is a shock to you."

"We haven't spoken...we were sixteen years old..." Amanda stared at her cousin as if the woman were a strange riddle. "Oh my...it's been years on top of years..."

"Do you still hate me?" Julie asked, her voice strained.

"Why are you here in Snow Falls?" Amanda asked, barely able to speak.

Julie dropped her eyes. "My husband and I are divorced. My son is currently refusing to speak to me. You're the only family I have left. I decided it was time to put the past away and...well, here I am."

Amanda watched a tear fall from Julie's eye. "Oh my. Sarah, it looks like we have two broken hearts to take care of." Amanda hurried over to her cousin and offered a loving hug. "I don't hate you, love. I never hated you. We were only sixteen years old. I forgave you years and years ago...oh, you poor dear."

Bethany wasn't sure what to say or do. She felt Sarah pull her close. "Sarah...this is all too much. I need...to be alone." She looked around and spotted an open office door. "Excuse me."

She hurried into Andrew's office, closed the office door, and bowed her head to pray. "Dear Lord...help me...I can't do this alone...I'm so scared...give me the strength to fight...one last fight, dear Lord...give me the strength."

"Is that woman alright?" Julie asked Amanda.

"No, but she will be," Amanda answered. She looked at Sarah with worried eyes. "Looks like we're going to have a very difficult winter, Los Angeles. We better get nestled in right here and now."

Sarah nodded in agreement. "Yes, it's going to be a very cold, hard, difficult winter," she agreed, then focused on Julie. Julie stared at her with uneasy eyes filled with broken tears. *Now we have two broken hearts to get through a difficult winter. Phew, what a winter this is going to be. But before winter can even begin, we have a killer to catch.*

Far away, the man who'd slipped a deadly poison into a batch of cinnamon buns walked into a warm cabin and spotted his grandfather sitting in a rocking chair beside a blazing fire.

"Grandfather McCrandy, it's sure coming down outside. Here's the wood."

Edwin McCrandy dropped a bucket full of firewood next to a stone fireplace and began warming his frozen hands.

chapter five

Edwin McCrandy made a thoughtful, concerned expression as Conrad Spencer spoke. "Yes, I read about the death of Greg Cranmore, detective," he told Conrad as he stood near a warm fireplace.

Conrad simply nodded without paying too much attention to Edwin. Edwin, Conrad saw, was a man in his late forties who resembled a soap opera actor—one of those guys who pretended his poop didn't stink because he walked around playing make-believe. Edwin had dark black hair that was slowly easing toward the gray side. The man's face was chiseled with sharp features that were beginning to show signs of aging. But what most caught Conrad's attention were Edwin's eyes—cold, malicious eyes that appeared soulless and evil.

"Mr. McCrandy," Conrad continued, speaking directly to Edwin's grandfather, "Andrew told me he had to ticket Brian Amerson for hunting on your land."

"Spotted that man on my land," John McCrandy spoke in a gruff voice without taking his eyes off the fireplace. He lifted a snuff can with a wrinkled hand and spat a bit of chewing tobacco juice into the can. John McCrandy reminded Conrad of a ninety-five-year-old Jimmy Stewart. "He used the old hunting path. Used to own his land. Sold it off when times got rough. Worst mistake I ever made."

Andrew leaned back against a thick wooden door, folded his arms, and surveyed a wide log living room that was more or less nothing more than a rustic room that held a couch, a rocking chair, and a wooden rack holding four hunting rifles. John McCrandy wasn't much on materialistic stuff. He was a simple man who loved the land. "We checked Brian Amerson's cabin, Mr. McCrandy. We didn't locate anything that seemed important. Have you seen any strangers around—"

"Haven't seen a soul," John cut Andrew off. "I'm ninety-five, but my eyes are still as sharp as an eagle's. Never wore glasses a day in my life. My ears can still hear a fieldmouse a mile away, too." He spat into the snuff can again. "You have to drive past my cabin to get to the land I sold. Even if you try to walk your way up, my old hunting dogs would bark up a storm. Just been me..." He tossed a thumb at Edwin. "My grandson here comes to visit me a lot. His daddy passed on thirty years ago. Bear mauled him to death. My grandson was eighteen at the time. Raised him up since then."

Something in John's voice didn't sit well with Conrad. It seemed he wasn't happy with his grandson. "Well, Mr. McCrandy, the snow is coming down pretty hard. We better get back into town," he told John. "If you see or hear anything, give me a call."

Edwin folded his arms over a gray sweater. "I have a home in Anchorage I'm currently selling, Detective Spencer. I'm planning to make Snow Falls my yearly residence. I...I'm certainly not pointing fingers, but it does seem to me that the two men who were murdered might somehow be related."

"We'll have to wait and see," Conrad informed Edwin. "Before I go, mind if I ask you a couple of questions?"

"Of course." Edwin unfolded his arms and placed them behind his back. "I completely support all law enforcement."

Conrad nodded. "What is your profession, Mr. McCrandy?"

"Politics. I have served on the Anchorage City Council for the last ten years. I also own two hotels in Anchorage," Edwin proudly answered.

"Are you married?" Conrad asked.

"I'm a widower," Edwin stated without showing an ounce of remorse. "My wife died two years after we married. The truck she was driving hit a patch of black ice. She crashed into a tree...the truck caught fire. I was thirty years old at the time. It's been some years."

"Are you in a relationship now?" Conrad continued.

Edwin shook his head. "I've been diagnosed with depression, Detective Spencer. I've decided to spend my years living in peace and quiet. You may not believe this, but living in Anchorage has been very hectic and stressful for me. All I want now is to walk in my grandfather's footsteps." He looked around him with his soulless eyes. "My grandfather owns two thousand acres of land. Someday, the land will be mine. I intend to love the land as much as my grandfather has. I also intend to live out my years in peace...a peace I desperately need."

Conrad glanced at John. The old man's eyes narrowed for a second, then cleared. *This guy has a nice speech going. He's full of hot air. Something is up with him...but what?* "Well, Snow Falls is a nice place to call home," he told Edwin. "That's all my questions. If I have more, I'll let you know." Conrad nodded at Andrew. "We better get back to town."

Andrew agreed. "See you later, Mr. McCrandy," he called out to John. "Maybe we can get some hunting in next month?"

"Maybe." John raised his left hand and waved at Andrew. "Tell the wife I said hello."

"Will do." Andrew opened the front door and walked

outside onto a snow-soaked front porch. He waited until Conrad joined him. "Yeah," he said, nodding his head.

"Yeah," Conrad said back. "That guy is a black spider." He tucked his head down against a screaming wind that was turning the snow into pieces of flying glass. "We can talk more once we're in my truck. Let's move."

Andrew fought his way down a pair of icy porch steps and stepped into knee-high snow. Conrad followed. "I'll do the driving," he called over his shoulder, scanning a white, frozen land that was quickly dimming as night came on. John's cabin was surrounded by thick, untamed woods filled with wild rivers and dangerous traps. "Old Man McCrandy lives a way up, Andrew!" he yelled, walking toward a gray truck that was parked behind a fancy Ford F-150. A 1948 pick-up truck was parked in front of the Ford. "Brian Amerson's land is north. Could never figure out why he was on Old Man McCrandy's land when he had all his land to hunt on?"

Conrad barely heard Andrew yelling over the wind. He kept his head tucked down and didn't say a word until he crawled into the cab of his truck. "Is there anything special on Mr. McCrandy's land?" he asked Andrew, blowing hot breath onto his gloved hands.

Andrew stationed himself behind a cold steering wheel. "No. Just an old mine that's been dry for over seventy years. Old Man McCrandy found a little gold in the mine back in his day. Way back, when the guy was in his twenties." Andrew brought Conrad's truck to life, clicked on the headlights, and focused on positioning the plow that was attached to the front of the truck in the right position.

"How much gold was found?"

"Just enough to buy four thousand acres of land, build a cabin, and have enough left over to live on," Andrew answered. He put Conrad's truck into four-wheel drive and put the gear into reverse. "I don't know the exact amount. My old man told me a few stories. He knew Old Man McCrandy. Went hunting with the guy a lot."

"Are you sure the mine is dry?" Conrad asked.

Andrew nodded as he backed down a snow-covered driveway, leaving a rustic cabin behind. "Trust me, Conrad, if that mine wasn't dry, every man in Alaska would be sneaking onto Old Man McCrandy's land. As a matter of fact, Old Man McCrandy ended up shooting a few people in his day just for that reason. Paul Winchester never arrested the guy for killing the trespassers. It was different in those days."

Conrad clicked on the front heater. "We need to figure out why Brian Amerson was trespassing on Mr. McCrandy's land."

"That's a good idea," Andrew agreed. "The man owned plenty of good hunting land." He reached the end of the driveway, backed up into a narrow, snow-covered dirt road, and kicked the gas. "Your plow is holding up good. We should reach town in good time."

Conrad nodded and dropped into a silent shadow as his thoughts began latching onto Edwin McCrandy. Andrew respected Conrad's silence. He dropped into his own thoughts as his hands navigated a tired truck back toward Snow Falls.

While Andrew pushed Conrad's truck through a hard snow, Bethany stepped out of his office. She spotted Amanda and Julie standing beside the coffee station, talking. Sarah was gone. Henry was sitting at one of the desks reading a fishing magazine. "Would it be alright if I had a cup of coffee?" she asked.

"Of course, love," Amanda told Bethany in a caring voice. "How are you feeling?"

"Oh...tired," Bethany admitted, walking over to the coffee

station. She looked at Julie with apologetic eyes. "I didn't mean to be rude earlier. I'm usually a friendly person—"

"Amanda explained everything. You have no need to apologize," Julie assured Bethany. "I'm terribly sorry. It seems like I showed up at the worst time. I should be the one apologizing."

Amanda poured Bethany a cup of coffee. "Here's some coffee in a funny Charlie Brown cup. Cheers, love."

Bethany accepted the coffee with two grateful hands. "I've been thinking," she spoke carefully. "I believe Greg Cranmore and Brian Amerson must be connected in some way. I'm not sure how. I'm also certain that the killer has been timing the murders."

Henry lowered the fishing magazine he was reading and glanced at Bethany. "How so?" he asked, curious.

"Both Greg Cranmore and Brian Amerson were killed shortly after interacting with me," Bethany explained, taking a sip of hot coffee. "The timing is too coincidental to be chance. Also," Bethany continued, "I think that both Greg Cranmore and Brian Amerson were sent to either intimidate or harm me. Both men were very upsetting to me."

"Love, that would mean the killer, whoever he is, must be targeting you," Amanda worried.

"Maybe not just me," Bethany told Amanda in a concerned tone. "Greg Cranmore warned me to stay away from you and Sarah. I think the entire reason for his visit was to try and make me stay away from you and Sarah."

"Why?" Amanda asked. She raised a stale donut and took a nibble. "What are your thoughts, love?"

"I'm not entirely certain," Bethany confessed. "But Amanda, I keep thinking about what Greg Cranmore told me."

"What did he tell you?" Henry stood up from his desk and walked over to the coffee station. He was intrigued.

"Well," Bethany stated in a thoughtful tone, "Greg

Cranmore told me that he was going to own Snow Falls someday. I remember Greg Cranmore becoming really upset with Sarah—"

"Because we bought O'Mally's. Yes, I know," Amanda sighed.

"Greg Cranmore said he had a developer set up..." Bethany took another sip of coffee. She preferred lots of cream and a little sugar in her coffee, but for the time being, sipping on a black coffee wasn't too horrible. "I'm not certain how Brian Amerson ties into this. If—and I'm simply assuming here—Brian Amerson was connected to Greg Cranmore, that could possibly mean the killer murdered them because some type of deal went sour, or maybe the killer is after some type of deal all for himself?"

"How does that involve you then?" Henry asked.

"A scapegoat," Bethany stated. "When you want to make everyone look right, you cause a distraction while you work with your left hand to carry out another objective. If everyone in town thinks I'm a killer, then the real killer has room to operate."

"That makes sense," Henry nodded. "But that still leaves us in the dark because we don't know who the killer is."

"Yes, that certainly is the problem, isn't it?" Bethany looked down at her coffee. "And I could be way off-base, too. I don't know how Nancy Drew remains sane."

A brown telephone on Henry's desk rang. "I'll answer that." Henry hurried to answer the call. "Oh Sarah...yeah, we were just talking...no cell phone service...yeah, the winds are fierce...one second." Henry held up the phone. "Amanda, it's Sarah."

"Thanks, love." Amanda handed Julie her stale donut and took the call.

Julie offered a weary smile. "Murder is an awful creature, isn't it?" she asked Bethany. "In London, I worked for a publishing house. I worked as an editor. I can't tell you how many manuscripts I read that involved murder...awful. Sadly, murder is what sells."

Bethany looked into Julie's face. Julie had a very sweet face, much like Amanda. Amanda didn't resemble Julie, though. Amanda looked like a pretty British actress while Julie resembled a nurse or a schoolteacher. "I wrote a book that involved murder," she told Amanda. "I regret writing a single word of that book. I wrote many children's books. I...I don't know what made me write a book about murder. I suppose I was very angry at my husband."

"It's good to vent," Julie told Bethany without casting any judgments. "Sometimes a woman has to vent. I spent an entire evening throwing plates against a tree."

"You did?"

"I drove to the countryside and broke ten sets of dishes," Julie explained. "Needless to say, I felt better afterward."

"Maybe I should have thrown dishes at a tree instead of writing a murder mystery book," Bethany moaned. "I certainly don't feel good about myself." She glanced around the police station. *Snow Falls is going to be my home. I can't give up the fight. I came to Snow Falls to start a new life and find peace. I can't run away, scared and frightened. I lived my life that way for twenty-one years. I have to start fighting. If I run away, I'll never stop running.* "We might as well make another pot of coffee. I have a feeling we're going to have a very long night."

"Okay, love, I got it...bye." Amanda ended the call with a shaking hand. She slowly turned around and looked at Bethany. "Sarah's been doing a bit of research, love. She has some bad news."

Bethany tensed up and waited for Amanda to throw a frozen snowball at her face.

"Greg Cranmore lived in Anchorage, Alaska before he moved to Snow Falls. He was being investigated for real estate fraud, but managed to avoid criminal charges," Amanda spoke clearly, paused, nibbled on a stale donut, and shot Henry a sour eye. Poor Henry simply sighed. Fred was the donut man, not him.

Amanda continued. "Brian Amerson lived in Snow Falls for the past ten years, like you said, love. But before he moved to Snow Falls, the sour bloke lived in Anchorage. And are you ready for the black eye?"

Bethany sighed. "I'm ready, Amanda."

Amanda tossed the stale donut she was holding into a wooden trash can. Her bottomless stomach apparently couldn't handle eating another stale donut. "Brian Amerson was business partners with Greg Cranmore."

"Now isn't that something," Henry whistled.

"Both of those blokes were in the real estate game," Amanda nodded. "Now they're dead."

"Which might imply—" Bethany began to speak.

"I think this discovery supports your theory," Henry firmly, but gently cut Bethany off. "Bethany, I think you've put a light in a dark tunnel here."

Bethany glanced around at the three caring, supportive faces. *I could be the killer, but the people staring at me trust I'm being honest. They truly care about me as friends. I have to find out what is happening in Snow Falls and prove my innocence, but also to help my friends. Somehow, I think Sarah and Amanda are in just as much danger as I am.* "You might be right, Henry...or wrong. We're still in the dark because we don't know who the killer is." Bethany focused on Amanda. "What else did Sarah say?"

"That's all she had...for now," Amanda asserted. "My dear friend is a woman who knows how to take a spoon and dig to London. If there is treasure to find, she'll find it."

"Yeah, Sarah is a pretty smart woman," Henry concurred. "Shame she retired from being a detective." Henry rubbed the back of a sore neck. "But I think Sarah is happier being a mother and running O'Mally's. Sure glad you two bought O'Mally's and kept the old place the same. I'm fond of that building."

"So am I, love," Amanda told Henry, and then lowered her eyes for a second. "Greg Cranmore did give a large dose of hostility toward Sarah and myself when Mr. O'Mally agreed to sell us the building and allowed us to keep his name. I can understand a bloke being angry because we stepped on his toes a little, but Greg Cranmore became a raging bull."

"I noticed he kept looking at Sarah with angry eyes when I was closing on my cabin and the coffee shop," Bethany added. "He told me he had a developer lined up—"

"To destroy O'Mally's and build a lousy chain of cheap stores probably," Henry grumbled. "O'Mally's sits just outside of town near the business district—if you can call a street lined with a few restaurants and a hotel a business district. But still..." Henry continued to rub the back of his neck as he thought. "The building sits on a few acres of open land that's connected to over one hundred acres of raw land that keeps running north into the wild. A greedy developer might see a great amount of potential, but folks in Snow Falls are conservative. We like to keep things simple and just the way they are."

Bethany soaked in Henry's words. *Could the killings be connected to some type of real estate deal? Could a hungry developer be after Snow Falls? Is that why Greg Cranmore was planted in Snow Falls?* "Henry, what happened to the last realtor in Snow Falls?" she asked.

"Oh, I can answer that, love," Amanda spoke up. "Mrs. Owens was the last realtor. She was eighty years old. Her children finally convinced her to retire and move to Fairbanks to be close to them. That was...oh...two years ago. Greg Cranmore showed up in town soon after."

Bethany rubbed her bottom lip. "I see."

"What is it?" Henry asked.

"Maybe Detective Spencer should call Mrs. Owens and ask if someone contacted her children? Maybe a threat was made?" Bethany suggested. "I could be wrong, but it seems strange that Greg Cranmore appeared in Snow Falls soon after Mrs. Owens left."

"Never connected those dots. You could be on to something," Henry told Bethany while nodding his head. "I never paid much attention to Greg Cranmore. Man never broke the law, and that was good enough for me."

Amanda began to speak, but stopped when Conrad and Andrew burst through the front door, covered with snow. "Whew, the wind is enough to cut a man in half!" Andrew called out, hurrying Conrad through the front door. "Any calls, Henry?" he asked, shoving the front door closed once Conrad was safely inside.

"Fred's wife hurt her ankle. He's at the hospital with her. It's just been me and these ladies for the past few hours," Henry explained. "Kick over any good rocks up there on the old Mine Road?"

Conrad quickly surveyed the front room. He spotted a strange woman standing close to Amanda. "I don't think I know you?" he asked Julie while shaking snow off his leather jacket.

"That's because you don't know my cousin, you silly bloke," Amanda scolded Conrad.

"Cousin?" Conrad asked. He was used to Amanda's fussy nature. She had become like a sister to him.

"My name is Julie Walsh," Julie politely introduced herself. "I...well, it certainly seems I showed up in Snow Falls at the wrong time. Two men are dead and now it seems I...well, I would think it strange, too, if a woman showed up after two men had been killed."

Bethany glanced over at Julie. *I didn't consider how Julie might be feeling, and how strange it is that she's in Snow Falls. It does seem strange that she showed up after the murder of Brian Amerson. But obviously the woman isn't a killer. She had bad timing, sure...but she isn't a killer. But who will believe that? Who will believe I'm not a killer? What a mess this is. So much for peace and quiet. All the lovely snow is being tainted with...murder.*

"Detective Spencer, your wife called while you were gone."

"Is everything alright?" Alarm struck Andrew's voice.

"Sarah did some research," Amanda spoke quickly, calming him down. "Here's the news." She asked Bethany and Julie to fix Conrad and Andrew a cup of coffee while she filled them in. Bethany and Julie jumped into action and worked to bring coffee to the two men who appeared frozen to the core.

"And that's about the gist of what Sarah has discovered so far," Amanda finished.

Conrad took a sip of hot coffee and thought for a few seconds. "I think Edwin McCrandy might be our man, Andrew."

"Who?" Henry asked.

"Edwin McCrandy," Andrew clarified. "Edwin McCrandy is John McCrandy's grandson...but remember, Old Man McCrandy is ninety-five. Edwin is a guy who looks like he's pushing fifty."

"A real snake," Conrad added. "The guy has snake eyes. Cold...lifeless." He took another sip of coffee, scanned the front room, and shook his head. "There's nothing more we can do tonight except use our brains to think and wait. The snow is falling too hard to move around in. We barely made it back to town. I think—"

The telephone sitting on Henry's desk rang.

"Just a second," Henry hurried to answer the call. "Snow Falls Police Station...oh, hey, Doc...yeah, he's right here." Henry held the phone out for Conrad.

"It's Doc Whitfield."

Conrad handed Andrew his coffee cup and took the call. "Yeah, Doc, what have you got for me? Yeah...that is strange...can't identify the poison?" Conrad shook his head.

"All the cinnamon rolls were laced with the poison, right...thought as much...had heart disease, huh...poison went straight to the heart and caused a massive heart attack...yeah, real clever..."

Bethany listened to Conrad speak to Dr. Whitfield, soaking in his every word. When he finished the call, she asked, "Am I under arrest?"

Conrad shook his head. "Of course not," he answered. "I think I know who the killer is, Ms. Lights. Now all I have to do is prove it. That's going to be the tough part. I think—"

The telephone sitting on Henry's desk rang again, cutting Conrad off for a second time. Conrad answered the call.

"Hello?"

"Yes, this is Edwin McCrandy, I need an ambulance. My grandfather has stopped breathing." Edwin's voice plowed into Conrad's ear the way a man might hear a snake hissing in the distance. "I found him slumped over in his rocking chair. Please, send an ambulance."

Conrad dropped his head. "The roads are impassable. It'll take a plow hours to get to your location. But hang tight and we'll get to you."

"Hurry," Edwin pressed. "I think my grandfather might have had a heart attack. I'm not sure."

"Have you tried CPR?"

"I don't know how to do CPR," Edwin confessed. "It's been years. Please, hurry."

"Alright, just sit right." Conrad put the phone down with an angry hand. "Edwin McCrandy...he said he found John McCrandy unresponsive...not breathing," he informed Andrew.

Andrew felt his cheeks turn redder than a hot fireplace iron. "If that snake killed Old Man McCrandy..." He set down the two coffee cups he was holding and rushed into his office. "Yeah, Mac, this is Andrew. Get your plow ready. We need to get up to the old Mine Road...I know it's snowing cats and dogs, Mac...meet me in ten. I need to call the hospital and get an ambulance ready...yeah, yeah, you'll get paid!"

Conrad quickly checked the time. "There's no need to rush, Andrew," he called out. "I have a bad feeling that John McCrandy is dead."

Henry bowed his head. "Old John...dead. I figured he'd outlive us all."

"My goodness," Julie whispered. "I left London because the city was becoming very hostile and violent, very corrupt. It seems like the fangs of evil are everywhere in the world now. There's not a safe place to hide."

No, there certainly isn't a safe place to hide anymore, Bethany thought, her mind struggling to connect a line of confusing dots. *I feel so helpless...I'm trapped in the snow. There's nothing I can do except wait.* "What a night this is turning out to be." With those words, she plopped down on a wooden chair and prepared to wait out a long night.

Conrad and Andrew waited until Mac showed up with his plow, and then fought their way back into the snowstorm, leaving the police station in Henry's hands again. Two hours later, Conrad called the station and asked to speak to Bethany.

"Yes, Detective Spencer, this is Bethany," she answered.

Conrad waited until two frustrated paramedics hauled John McCrandy's body outside into the snow before speaking. "Ms. Lights, I found a sweater in John McCrandy's bedroom that had a very distinct smell of perfume on it along with a note."

"A note? Perfume?" Bethany felt her heart begin to race.

"A half-finished note that John McCrandy was writing to you...at least, that's how it appears. And as far as the perfume smell on the sweater—"

"My perfume?" Bethany asked weakly.

"I'm afraid so," Conrad nodded. "The same perfume Amanda gave you for Thanksgiving. I remember the smell because Amanda sprayed the perfume around. It made me cough." Conrad spotted Edwin step through the open front door. "Yes, Henry, we're moving back toward town," he suddenly spoke in a tough cop tone. "Inform Dr. Whitfield that John McCrandy will be arriving DOA. Our ETA back to Snow Falls should be one hour. Put Bethany Lights in holding cell one."

Edwin watched Conrad slam down a brown telephone receiver with an angry hand. "What will you do, detective?" he asked in an upset voice. "Will you arrest that awful woman?"

"Yes," Conrad nodded. "It seems we found the killer." Conrad spotted Andrew step through the front door. "All set?" he asked his partner.

Andrew nodded yes. "Mac is ready," he spoke wearily. "Mr. Edwin, you will need to drive into town tomorrow and give an official statement. Considering the weather, I'm excusing you from having to drive into town tonight. But I will be expecting you tomorrow."

"My truck has a plow," Edwin assured Andrew, sounding distraught, yet very phony. "I'll try my best."

"Good enough." Andrew nodded at Conrad. "Let's move. The snow is coming down heavier by the second. Mac isn't going to wait all night."

Conrad eyed Edwin for a second and prepared to step outside into a war zone of icy winds and razor-sharp snow.

Edwin quickly closed and locked the front door behind him.

"Ms. Lights has just been set up for murder, Andrew," Conrad spoke, fighting his way through the deep snow while keeping his head tucked down. A dump truck with glowing lights was sitting close by, ready to move. A sharp, powerful plow was attached to the front of the dump truck, ready for action.

"I know." Andrew climbed into the passenger seat of Conrad's truck and waited. Once Conrad was situated behind the steering wheel, he let out an angry growl. "Conrad, we have to take this guy down! Three people are dead. How many more people are going to die, for goodness' sake?"

"I know we have to take Edwin McCrandy down." Conrad brought his truck to life. "The question is...how, Andrew? Bethany Lights is the one the courts will condemn right now." The truth of the matter was, Conrad had no idea how he was going to take down a clever killer. All he could do was put his truck in reverse and follow a tired ambulance and a worn-down dump truck. "Andrew, we're dealing with a vicious killer."

"That's it. Run away, you pathetic worms," Edwin grinned, watching Conrad's truck vanish into the snow. "You'll never catch me. I put a pillow over the old man's face and you'll never be able to prove it. And as far as Bethany Lights is concerned...well, all eyes are on her now. But don't worry, detective, soon I'll be going after your wife and her little friend. But for now, I'll focus on ensuring that Bethany Lights takes a very hard fall before I kill her." Edwin let out a pleased laugh and moved away from the front door, walking toward a warm fire. "Soon, Ms. Lights, you'll be dead."

What Edwin McCrandy didn't know—what nobody knew —was that there was another killer hiding in the snow, silent and unseen, waiting to strike.

Bethany Lights was the main target.

chapter six

Morning arrived. A dim, gray light cast life onto a snow-soaked town that was sitting under a heavy blanket of snow. Not a single person was out and moving. For the time being, Snow Falls was completely snowed under.

The residents of Snow Falls were not concerned. They were used to heavy snowstorms. Folks simply stayed inside their homes and snuggled up to a warm fireplace. Soon the plows would be moving and life would start to defrost, as always. There was no rush to move the snow and dig out frozen trucks. The blanket of heavy snow covering Snow Falls offered a peaceful hug that transformed the town into a sleepy, beautiful winter wonderland that the outside world could not touch or harm. No one was in a hurry to escape the peaceful slumber enveloping their home...except for Bethany Lights. Bethany was anxious to catch a deadly killer.

"Mac will have the plows moving soon," Andrew yawned, rubbing a face that was obviously very exhausted. "This is Snow Falls, Bethany. Whenever we get snowed under, we wait a while and eventually Mac clears the roads."

"Mac has a ten-man team. Snow Falls has numerous roads," Conrad pointed out, fighting back a yawn. "The city roads are cleared first, and then Mac and his team head out into the county. It takes time."

"Blimey, it takes all day," Amanda complained, chugging down a cup of hot coffee. "And stop with the city and county talk, you bloke. Snow Falls isn't like some town in the lower states. Snow Falls is special...connected...one heart. I don't like to hear you break my home down into technical terms."

"Are we a bit grumpy?" Conrad teased Amanda.

Amanda raised a fist into the air. "Don't make me punch you into last year!" she warned Conrad.

Conrad rolled his sleepy eyes. Amanda was something else. "Alright, alright, calm down. I'm sorry."

Bethany ignored Amanda and Conrad's war. Her mind was focused on Edwin McCrandy. "Detective Spencer, I read the note you found at John McCrandy's home. I'm in very serious trouble."

"We have to have the handwriting on the note analyzed," Conrad pointed out. "I seriously doubt if John McCrandy wrote that note, Bethany. Anyone can try to forge another person's handwriting."

"What about my perfume?" Bethany asked, staring at the front door of the police station. *I placed the perfume Amanda gave me for Thanksgiving on the nightstand in my bedroom. Someone was in my bedroom...in my cabin. And I wasn't even aware of it.* "When I left home yesterday morning, the perfume Amanda gave me was sitting on my nightstand. I wonder if the perfume is still there?"

"We'll check," Andrew replied. Boy, was he ever sleepy. Andrew was the type of man that needed a solid eight hours of sleep each night or he was no good the next day. Sometimes, police work stunk rotten eggs.

"The note John McCrandy supposedly wrote contained the names of Greg Cranmore and Brian Amerson. Supposedly, John McCrandy was writing me a warning note, telling me to leave town until the heat died down."

"'Leave town for a bit. You can't kill two men and not expect the cops to start sniffing around,'" Conrad quoted a line from the note he found in John McCrandy's bedroom. "The note also specified how you were tied into a corrupt real estate deal with Greg Cranmore and Brian Amerson. John McCrandy, it seems, was taken aback by your beauty, Bethany, and was willing to turn his land over to you."

Bethany sighed. "I'm being set up for murder." *Whoever this Edwin McCrandy crumb is, he's doing a good job at setting me up. I'm going to have a hard time proving my innocence.* "I did make several visits to Snow Falls in the past," she told Conrad. "I never spoke to anyone. I wasn't even sure what I was doing in Snow Falls or if I truly had the courage to move here. This was before my husband was killed. I knew he was preparing to divorce me. I was searching for a new life." She sighed. "I always visited during the spring and summer months. When you check the hotel, you'll find records of my past visits—four total."

Conrad felt a headache scream his name. Bethany was in a world of trouble. Technically, he was supposed to put the woman under arrest, but how could he? Bethany was innocent and Edwin McCrandy was the killer. Proving both points was going to be the hard part. "Dr. Whitfield told me that the poison that killed Brian Amerson was designed to attack the heart through the digestive tract. I did some checking and found out that Edwin McCrandy attended the University of Iowa in his earlier years. He majored in political science, but I had Sarah dig even deeper for me. Sarah discovered that Edwin had a friend who majored in chemistry. The friend in question is now dead. Supposedly, the friend killed himself."

Bethany swung around to face Conrad. The sudden news seemed to ignite a little flame of hope in her depressed heart. Amanda, Julie, Andrew, and Henry all stepped closer to Conrad. "Is there anything else?" Bethany pressed.

Conrad shrugged his tired shoulders. "The friend was found dead in Anchorage. His body was found in a rental cabin by a cabin-cleaning company. Anchorage police ruled the death a 'Clear Suicide,' which means the case is closed." He shook his head. "Sarah confirmed that the guy—his name was Robbie Malone, by the way, age forty-nine—was recently divorced and had been fired from his job at the Taswell Medical Corporation. Robbie Malone was a chemist."

"A dead stiff can't talk," Andrew mumbled under his breath.

"A suicide letter was found in the cabin," Conrad finished. "Robbie Malone killed himself by drinking a bottle of poison. His wishes were to be cremated. His wife carried out the guy's wish as soon as an official autopsy was performed and the police ruled the death a 'Clear Suicide.'"

"Bet the poison in question is the same poison that killed Brian Amerson," Andrew insisted.

"Probably. But the only problem is, Dr. Whitfield told me the poison that killed Brian Amerson is a fast-dissolving agent that seems to rapidly clear out of the bloodstream and major arteries." Conrad walked over to the coffee station and poured himself a cup of coffee. He stared at the cup for a minute, then turned to face Bethany. "You attended college."

"And I majored in English and had a minor in chemistry," Bethany confirmed, feeling her heart drop. "I began studying medicine, but quickly changed my major after I realized I couldn't stand the sight of blood."

"Which means you have a clear understanding of human anatomy," Conrad pointed out. She nodded. "Someone dug into your past, Bethany, and snatched up some good dirt on you. That someone is Edwin McCrandy. I believe—"

A sleepy telephone rang. Henry hurried to answer the call. "One second, Doc...it's Doc Whitfield."

Conrad took the call with a calm hand. "John McCrandy suffocated to death, didn't he?" he asked Dr. Whitfield.

"Well," an old voice creaked, standing in a lonely basement room next to a dead body, "I can't say for sure if that's the case, Conrad. All I can say is that I found small traces of lint in John's nose and in his mouth. For all intents and purposes, it would seem the man died of a heart attack. I found no injuries on him except a few old bruises. If John had put up a struggle before he was killed, there is no evidence."

Conrad rubbed his forehead with a frustrated hand. "Throw a pillow over the victim's body with one hand while holding another pillow over the victim's face..."

"Could be," Dr. Whitfield agreed. "Proving such a thing will be impossible, Conrad. And as far as the lint I found...well, anyone who rolls over on his pillow while asleep can breathe in small traces of lint. Lint builds up over time...well, you get my point."

"Dr. Whitfield, did you find any traces of a woman's perfume on John McCrandy?" Conrad asked.

"No," Dr. Whitfield answered. "But it's strange you ask because I did find some pencil lead on the inside of John's right palm. Maybe John had been writing a letter? I can't say for sure. The traces of lead I found were very small, just a little smudge, really. John was a very old man."

Conrad nodded. "A man who was killed, and I'm going to prove it. Thanks, Dr. Whitfield. I'll be in touch."

"I know you will," Dr. Whitfield informed Conrad in a voice that became very tired. "You know I never involved myself in police business, Conrad. But I heard two of the nurses last night talking about how they believe Bethany Lights killed two innocent men. Enough said."

"Thanks, Dr. Whitfield." Conrad ended the call with a weary hand. "Bethany, I want you to spend the day here at the police station. You're not under arrest, but I am asking you remain in custody for your own protection. In the meantime, I'm going to use the snowmobile out back,

Andrew, and get home to my wife and daughter. I'll be back after lunch."

"I better call my hubby to come and get me," Amanda informed everyone. "I'm pooped to pop, as you yanks say. I need some sleep." She turned to Bethany. "Sarah will be along shortly, love."

"Mind if I go home with you?" Julie asked Amanda.

"Of course not." Amanda squeezed Julie's hand. "We have a lot to talk about and a lot to do." She offered her cousin a warm, loving smile. "Everything is going to be alright. Wait and see."

Maybe for Julie, but not for me. I'm in deep trouble. Eventually, Conrad is going to have to contact the state and make an arrest. My time is short. He can't protect me forever. And it won't be long, I suppose, before Edwin McCrandy begins to demand Conrad arrest me for the murder of Greg Cranmore and Brian Amerson. While I was blindly focusing on starting my new life in Snow Falls, Edwin McCrandy was working behind the scenes, in the shadows, to destroy my life. Bethany felt a surge of panic strike her worried heart. *I need a plan. But what? How am I going to outsmart a killer? Think, Bethany…it's time to fight.*

"Conrad, would it be alright if I spent the day at my coffee shop?" she asked.

"Why?" Conrad asked uncertainly.

"You told me that Edwin McCrandy is supposed to drive into town today and give a statement. I don't want to be here when that awful man arrives."

Conrad had not taken into consideration how Bethany might feel when Edwin showed up at the police station. He glanced at Andrew. "Andrew?"

"I'll have Henry close to Ms. Lights," Andrew yawned. "Andy will be along shortly. I'll stay around until Edwin McCrandy arrives, then I'll go home and get some rest." Andrew looked at poor Henry. "Mind babysitting today?"

Henry shook his head. "I don't mind at all." He stepped

close to Bethany. "I know you're innocent, Bethany. A man my age has a way of knowing these things. I'm going to stand by you. You got a friend in me and my wife."

"Thank you, Henry." Bethany reached out and squeezed his hand. "You're a blessing."

Henry blushed a little. "Just doing what the Good Lord would have me do is all."

Bethany smiled and hurried to put on her coat. "It'll be good for me to walk down to my coffee shop before the roads are plowed. I don't want anyone to see me out and about."

Henry threw on his coat and a brown muffler hat. "I'll holler if there's a problem," he told Andrew.

Andrew hesitated for a second. Would Bethany try to leave Snow Falls? Would she harm Henry? Was she really a killer? The cop side of Andrew wanted to throw a million and one practical questions at Bethany, but the human side of Andrew—his heart—told him Bethany was as innocent as a doe walking through a fresh blanket of snow in a sleeping forest. "I'll be here."

"Be careful, love," Amanda pleaded with Bethany. "You have my cell phone and my house phone."

"I do." Bethany hugged Amanda. "Thank you for staying with me. I'm so very grateful." She turned her eyes to Julie. "I hope we get the chance to become friends."

"Me too," Julie told Bethany, offering a supportive hug. "Be careful."

Bethany hugged Julie back and asked Henry to open the front door. As soon as he pulled the front door open, a powerful, screaming wind rushed into the police station. Bethany quickly shielded her eyes and stepped out into knee-deep snow. *At least the snow has stopped falling for now. The plows should be out soon, and that's what I want. I have a plan...a very dangerous plan, but I can't sit back and wait for Conrad and Andrew to save me. This is Snow Falls, and in Snow Falls, I'm learning that a woman has to save herself.*

Bethany began a difficult walk through the deep snow while keeping her head down against the icy winds. Snow Falls was completely covered by a white blanket of snow—a beautiful winter wonderland that captivated Bethany's heart. *This little town is so beautiful. The snow is beautiful. The winds are harsh, but that's alright. I'm where I belong. I feel that truth in my heart. I have to fight. I'm not going to let Edwin McCrandy drag my life into a dark closet.*

"You okay?" Henry yelled over the screaming winds.

"I'm okay!"

"Keep your head tucked down and keep moving. Snow is deep. Stay away from the drifts!" He warned.

Bethany nodded and worked her way down a frozen sidewalk. When she reached the Snow Falls bakery, she heard an eerie voice whisper, *Scrooge…Scrooge…Scrooge…*

Bethany stopped moving and looked into the front window of the bakery. As she did, the face of a very scared-looking man appeared. The man was standing next to a foggy grave, begging for his life. *Can a person truly be redeemed?* Bethany wondered, staring into the bakery window. *I wrote an awful book. In the book, I killed my husband…I'm not innocent. My heart is still filled with anger…and yes, even hate. Perhaps I am Ebenezer Scrooge—only, there is no redemption for me. Maybe this is my punishment for writing such an awful book? I guess I'll find out. Right now, I just have to keep fighting my way forward.*

Bethany drew in an icy breath of air and forced her legs to start moving again—moving through a deep snow she feared might become her grave.

"You want to *what?*" Henry almost hit the floor.

"I want to call Edwin McCrandy," Bethany explained as she poured Henry a cup of hot coffee. "I know Detective Spencer and Andrew—and Sarah—would not approve. But

Henry, you and I both know Detective Spencer and Andrew have to work within the barriers of the law. I don't."

"I do," Henry pointed out, accepting his cup of coffee. "Bethany, I'm still sworn to uphold the law."

Bethany poured herself a cup of coffee and stared deep into Henry's eyes. "Henry, what if Snow Falls didn't have a police department? When our forefathers journeyed to America from Europe, they didn't arrive in a land that had police stations. They had to slowly establish what we call the law today. If a person broke an established law our forefathers saw as right, that person was swiftly punished." She bit her lower lip. "Henry, Andrew told me that a man or woman has to be prepared to defend his or her life in Snow Falls. I'm taking him up on those words."

Henry took a nervous sip of coffee. Fire was burning in Bethany's eyes, and he knew well enough to let a woman burn through a forest before trying to throw cold water on her. "Well, for goodness' sakes, why do you want to call Edwin McCrandy? That sour skunk is a killer, Bethany."

"Exactly!" Bethany looked down at her feet. Her dear friend the raccoon was back in his doggy bed. "Henry, I need to lure Edwin McCrandy into my coffee shop. When the time is right, you'll pounce on him and make a justifiable arrest."

"After you do what?" Henry dared to press.

"Make a murderer confess to killing three men," Bethany explained.

"Well, how in the world do you plan to do that?" Henry swallowed a gulp of hot coffee. "What I need is one of those good cinnamon buns Sarah and Amanda used to make."

"Bingo!" Bethany yelled so loudly that Henry nearly fell off his wooden stool. "Henry, the cinnamon buns are going to be the weapon I use to make Edwin McCrandy confess to his crimes."

"Come again?" Henry stared at Bethany as if the woman had done lost her living, loving mind.

"You'll see," Bethany promised. She reached out her right hand and touched Henry's arm. "Henry, please, if I don't do this, I'm afraid Edwin McCrandy might strike first. I have a very bad feeling I might be his next target. I have to act, and Detective Spencer and Andrew...well, Henry, they can't help me. I know they're both trying, but they can't help me. A woman just knows."

Henry stared into Bethany's desperate eyes for a minute. "Yeah, guess a woman does know. When my wife gets a gut feeling, well, whatever she's feeling always seems to come to pass." Henry patted Bethany's arm. "I'm on your side, Bethany. Like I said last night, you got a friend in me and my wife."

"Oh, thank you, Henry!" Bethany reached across the counter and hugged Henry, nearly spilling the man's coffee.

"You can thank me after I arrest a killer," Henry told Bethany, hugging her back.

Bethany drew in a deep breath and checked the time. "Conrad called the police station last night using a landline phone that's in John McCrandy's cabin. I need to call that phone."

"I've got the number," Henry confessed reluctantly. "Reckon we best get on with your plan."

Bethany eyed a brown telephone sitting on the front counter. She drew in a courageous breath, whispered an urgent prayer, and picked up the receiver. "Alright, Henry, I'm ready. Give me the number."

Henry steadied a stiff coffee cup, then spoke the dangerous phone number into Bethany's ears. She nervously dialed each number.

chapter seven

Edwin was opening the front door of John McCrandy's cabin when an old telephone sitting on a rustic coffee table rang. He nearly ignored the call, but something told him to leave the front door closed. "Who could be calling?" he grumbled. "I'm dressed and ready to go into town. I don't have time to be annoyed." He stared at the ringing telephone for a second, and then marched across the living room.

"Hello?" he nearly snapped.

Bethany forced her heart to remain in her chest. "Mr. McCrandy, this is Bethany Lights. I believe you are out to kill me? I think we need to talk before I help the police send you to prison for killing Greg Cranmore and Brian Amerson."

Edwin froze. He felt his entire body turn into a lump of ice. His mind suddenly drew a blank as his legs stiffened into frozen pieces of wood. "I don't know what you're talking about," he finally managed to speak.

"Yes, you do," Bethany declared. "You poisoned the cinnamon buns in my coffee shop. The police took every cinnamon bun except for one. I had a cinnamon bun in my office. I told the police I fed the cinnamon bun to a raccoon. I lied." Bethany glanced at Henry, who simply folded his arms together and listened. "You poisoned Brian Amerson."

The last thing in the world Edwin had expected was to receive a call from Bethany Lights. And to make matters more complicated, Bethany was stating facts that could send Edwin to prison...for life. "You're insane!"

"Am I?" Bethany asked, deciding it was time to slap Edwin across his face. "Mr. McCrandy, I'm going to dedicate the rest of my life to proving you killed Greg Cranmore and Brian Amerson...and possibly John McCrandy. I'm also going to prove you were connected to a very corrupt real estate deal."

Edwin felt as if a hard fist had burst through the phone and punched him in the gut. "You're mentally deranged—"

"Tell that to Brian Amerson. Before the man died in front of me, he mentioned you by name, Mr. McCrandy. Why? Because Brian Amerson had plans of his own and I used a little...ingenuity...to make him talk. You see, Mr. McCrandy, I'm not a stupid woman. When Greg Cranmore turned up dead, I knew something was wrong. When Brian Amerson showed up in my coffee shop to kill me—and he was sent by you to do the job—I was prepared. I had a hidden camera all ready. After Brian threatened me, I revealed the camera and showed Greg Cranmore a live camera feed that was connected to a private online blog. Needless to say, the man quickly broke. It's a shame he died. You were smart to poison the cinnamon buns."

"You're lying!" Edwin erupted.

"Dare to see my blog? I can send you a copy of Greg Cranmore's visit." Bethany closed her eyes. *Can I really bluff a killer? I'm about to find out. I'm putting my life on the line, but that's the risk I have to take. If I'm going to make Snow Falls my home, I'm going to have to catch Edwin McCrandy myself and prove to everyone that I'm innocent. I know Detective Spencer and Andrew are trying to help, but there comes a time when a woman knows what she has to do.* "I can send a copy...or I can remain silent...for a price."

"For a price?" Edwin asked, struggling to focus.

"Money, Mr. McCrandy," Bethany clarified. "Come to my coffee shop and we'll set up a monthly payment plan that will allow me to...remain silent, if you will. But I swear, if you try to harm me...if I end up dead...three people have a copy of Brian Amerson confessing to me that you sent him to kill me. The tape will go public faster than you can blink. Your only option is to agree to pay me. And now that John McCrandy is dead, you'll inherit quite a bit of land...at least that's what I overheard Detective Spencer telling someone this morning. You can sell the land and pay me."

Edwin felt his left hand form a deadly fist. Bethany Lights was a dead woman. He didn't know how he was going to kill her without the woman sending a damaging tape into the public sphere, but he would figure out a way. "What time do you want to meet?"

"In one hour. My coffee shop," Bethany demanded. "I'll have my hidden camera set up, so no funny stuff. Three sets of eyes will be watching from the lower states." She opened her eyes. *I can't believe I'm doing this. I must be insane...or maybe I've watched too many episodes of* Murder, She Wrote. "I'm not a stupid woman, Mr. McCrandy. I may seem weak and timid, but I assure you, after suffering through twenty-one years of a horrible marriage, I've learned to be a very smart fighter. You have one hour. I'll be waiting."

"Well, I'll be a monkey's butt!" Henry exclaimed as soon as Bethany ended the call. "You sounded like a real-life criminal. I'd swear you have a criminal running through your blood, Bethany. My goodness. I've never heard anything like this in my life. You carried out your lines so well, too."

Bethany lifted a shaky hand. "My voice may have sounded convincing, but I was shaking the entire time." She picked up her coffee cup and took three quick sips in order to calm her nerves. "Now we have to hurry and put the camera up."

"You mean, there really is a camera?" Henry asked.

"No, but we have to make Edwin McCrandy believe there is. Wait here." Bethany rushed into the kitchen. Five minutes later, she returned carrying a white dummy camera. "I found this camera in the back office. Sarah said she bought it to put on the outside of the back door. It's a dummy camera, but notice how realistic the camera looks."

Henry studied the camera Bethany was holding in her hands. "Well, the camera does look very real," he had to admit. "Why didn't Sarah put the camera up?"

"She had Little Sarah before she could," Bethany explained. *It's now or never. I've invited a killer to visit my coffee shop. I can't turn back now.* "Henry, please put this camera up in the far right corner." She pointed to the north wall. "There is a small toolbox under the front counter. There are some screws in the toolbox Sarah left me. Do what you can."

"What will you be doing?" Henry asked.

"Baking a cinnamon bun," Bethany answered. "One single cinnamon bun that's going to force a killer to admit his crimes. At least, I pray so." She studied the front room. "When you finish installing the camera, hide behind the front counter and stay out of sight."

"Andrew is going to throw me in jail and hide the keys," Henry moaned. "I must be out of my mind, but I reckon since the flood gates have opened, I better play along." He reached down and pulled a Glock 17 from a black police utility belt. "Yep, she's loaded and ready to go," he told Bethany, checking his gun. "Sam never lets me down."

"Sam?" Bethany asked.

"Sure. A fella has to name his gun," Henry insisted. "And speaking of gun—"

"Right here." Bethany reached under the front counter and pulled out her Glock 19. "I've spent countless hours at the firing range," she told Henry, checking her gun. "I know how to use my Glock better than I know how to drive a car."

Henry watched Bethany check a full clip. It appeared she knew how to handle her gun. That was good. "Keep your gun—"

"Under the counter and within reach." Bethany placed her gun back under the front counter. "Henry," she stated in a careful voice, "when I say the word 'snowman' three times, jump into action and make your arrest. But please, don't act until you hear me say the word 'snowman' three times."

"Snowman three times. I've got it," Henry promised. He offered a weary smile and laughed a little. "You know, Bethany, you remind me of Jane Wyatt from the old television show *Father Knows Best*. I always liked that show. And if you've ever seen the show, you'd know that Jane Wyatt's character was a simple, quiet, tender housewife who didn't look mean enough to step on a house spider. But you...even though you look meek and mild...well, I declare you have a tiger in you."

Bethany bowed her head. "Henry," she spoke, her voice broken, "you're the first man besides my daddy—rest his soul —that's ever been this kind to me. Here I am, asking you to risk your life and your career for a woman you barely know, and you're supporting me instead of condemning me. I really don't know what to say or how to ever thank you."

Henry stood up from his stool and pointed at Bethany. "Raise those eyes and look at me," he ordered. She looked up. "Now you listen to me, Bethany. God loves you just as much as He loves anyone else, and God commands us to love each other. That's what Jesus teaches us in the Bible. I take God's Holy Word very seriously, too. Now, I can clearly see you took some hard punches in your life, but that don't mean all people are bad and ugly, and it don't mean you can't be cared about." Henry softened his voice. "I took a liking to you the first minute I saw you because I can see goodness in you. Lots of pain, but goodness. And that's why I'm standing here. I don't plan to leave your side, either. Now, you best go bake that cinnamon bun and let me get to work."

A tear slipped from Bethany's eye. "Thank you, Henry," she managed to whisper, and then rushed away into the back kitchen.

"Okay...need to bake a cinnamon bun...and get ready to bluff a killer. I can do this. It's the only way I'm ever going to have peace in Snow Falls. Edwin McCrandy has to be captured." *If Daddy were alive today, he would have me admitted to a mental hospital...or maybe if Daddy were alive he would be out front, helping Henry put up a dummy camera.*

"Well, Daddy, here goes nothing." Bethany slapped on an apron and went to work preparing a single cinnamon bun.

Far away, Edwin McCrandy climbed into a fancy truck and prepared to drive into Snow Falls. "You're a dead woman, Ms. Lights. I don't know how I'm going to kill you...but I will. One way or another, by the time night arrives, you'll be dead."

Back in Snow Falls, a hidden killer remained out of sight and carefully watched Bethany's coffee shop with deadly eyes.

chapter eight

Edwin McCrandy stepped into Bethany's coffee shop like a man easing into the den of a sleeping grizzly bear. The first thing his murderous eyes noticed was a white camera perched in the far right corner of the front room like a stealthy snow owl waiting for a field mouse. A red light was glowing on the side of the camera. Edwin gritted his teeth as he closed the front door with a hand covered by a black glove.

Bethany was standing behind the front counter, her hands placed behind her back.

"Are we alone?" Edwin asked through gritted teeth.

Bethany took in the sight of an ugly, vicious killer. The amazing part was that Edwin McCrandy was actually quite handsome and intelligent in appearance. But beneath the man's façade, Bethany knew, the horrible killer was lurking.

"We're alone...in a sense." Bethany nodded toward the white dummy camera. "Please keep your hands away from your pockets and where I can see them at all times. Three people are watching us. If you make one wrong move, they will immediately call the Snow Falls Police Department. Also —" she jerked her arm, presenting her Glock 19. "I will not hesitate to shoot."

If Edwin could have strangled Bethany on the spot, he would have. No one—especially some dimwitted woman—ever talked down to him, let alone threatened to kill him. He was a man who always took charge of any situation, outsmarting every opponent and destroying every enemy. Bethany was a nuisance that had to be tended to with vicious intent, and nothing more. For the moment, he would lead the woman into believing she was in control...but only for the moment.

"May I sit down?"

"Sit down on the stool with the white duct tape on it," Bethany ordered.

Edwin spotted a wooden stool that indeed had a piece of white duct tape attached to it. He nodded, stomped snow off a pair of black boots, and brushed at the shoulders of a thick black coat. "It's beginning to snow some," he stated coldly as he approached the assigned stool.

Bethany carefully watched Edwin take his seat. "Place your hands on the counter. Fold them together, and leave them folded," she ordered, keeping her voice stern and calm, even though her heart was shaking like a leaf caught in a bitter autumn wind. Edwin hesitated, but obeyed. "Do not unfold your hands."

"Can we get on with business?" Edwin hissed, feeling his patience grow very thin. He did not like being treated like a stray dog.

"You have a hidden tape recorder in your coat pocket," Bethany told Edwin. Before he could answer, Bethany aimed the gun she was holding directly at the man's chest. "Yes or no. The right answer will keep you alive."

Edwin froze. His eyes locked on the face of a woman who clearly would not hesitate to shoot him dead. It was at that very second Edwin McCrandy realized he had dangerously underestimated Bethany Lights. She was not some weak, stupid woman he could kill without worry whenever his murderous heart decided to do so. She was a clever, strong, and determined woman—a fighter with the heart of a wounded lion refusing to go down without letting out one last mighty roar. "Yes, I have a tape recorder."

Bethany nodded without lowering her gun hand. She slowly slipped her left hand beneath the counter and retrieved a green plate holding a cinnamon bun. Poor Henry lay silent at Bethany's feet, watching her every move while ignoring the sleeping raccoon next to him. The blasted raccoon was just sleeping away without any concern whatsoever.

"I have a treat for you, Mr. McCrandy. I have a single cinnamon bun the police didn't take. I want you to eat it for me."

"What?" Edwin nearly fell off the stool he was sitting on. His blood went cold, falling into a deep ice pit.

"You will have two choices, Mr. McCrandy," Bethany spoke in a tone that sounded lifeless and cruel, a tone that worried Henry. "You can either walk out of here alive or dead. If you refuse to eat this cinnamon bun, I will simply shoot you. That is the first choice I'm offering you."

"What is the second choice?" Edwin heard his voice ask from a terrified, faraway place as his mind began to wonder how Bethany Lights had outsmarted him. No one outsmarted Edwin McCrandy!

"Confess to the murders of Greg Cranmore, Brian Amerson, and John McCrandy," Bethany stated, keeping her gun aimed at Edwin. "I know you killed those three men. Either confess to your guilt, or die."

Bethany's eyes clearly informed Edwin he was a dead man if he dared refuse to admit he was a deadly killer. His eyes dropped to the front right pocket of his black coat that was slowly changing into a prison uniform. "I have money—"

"Admit to the murders first," Bethany demanded. "If you

refuse, you will either eat that cinnamon bun or be shot. You decide your fate, Mr. McCrandy."

Edwin's eyes slithered over to the cinnamon bun sitting on the front counter like a dying snake that had been run over while trying to escape a hot road. The bun turned into the mouth of a raging monster screaming his name. For the first time in his life, Edwin McCrandy was trapped.

"How much money do you want?" he asked in a voice that, to Bethany's relief, started to tremble and break, like an iceberg breaking apart in a hot sun.

"Confess to the murders first. Those are the rules," Bethany demanded.

"I..." Edwin licked his lips. He looked up into Bethany's eyes. Her eyes told him to confess or die. "Yes, alright, you know I killed Greg Cranmore and Brian Amerson. I also killed…my grandfather, John McCrandy. I shot Greg Cranmore to death. I sneaked into this coffee shop and laced a batch of cinnamon buns with poison…Brian had a sweet tooth. I ordered Brian to kill you. I put a pillow over my grandfather's face. They all had to die!"

"Why?" Bethany asked without skipping a beat, struggling to hide how much heart was racing. She felt like passing out.

Edwin watched as Bethany's finger added pressure to a very delicate trigger. "Wait! I…I'll tell you," he cried out.

"I don't have all day, Mr. McCrandy." *I broke him. My plan actually worked. I bluffed a killer. I took a dangerous chance, but I bluffed a killer and won…by God's grace alone. Now all I have to do is make the monster sitting before me confess to a motive and Henry can make the arrest. Whew, what a morning.*

"Gold," Edwin blurted out, fearing for his life. Now that he was on the opposite end of the gun, fear—fear that seemed to suck the very life out of his heart—latched onto his soul with hungry teeth. He began to taste raw copper forming in his mouth, a sickening taste that made him want to vomit.

"The mine on my grandfather's land. The mine is still full of gold."

"How do you know that?" Bethany asked.

"I found one of my grandfather's journals," Edwin admitted, despising every breath Bethany took. "I read his secrets. The foolish old man was hiding the truth. All these years, I believed that mine was dull. My grandfather even sold off half his land. He claimed times were hard, but his actions were to deceive everyone, including me."

"And?" Bethany pressed.

Edwin locked his eyes on the cinnamon bun sitting on the counter. "I hired a mining expert—Brian Amerson. Brian confirmed that the mine still had gold in it, but it would require a great deal of blasting. There's a huge wall of rock that had to be removed. The rock is massive—miles wide in all directions. My grandfather dug a narrow underground tunnel underneath the rock, miles and miles. I can't imagine how many years it took him to dig that tunnel. The tunnel ends right under O'Mally's department store—it dead ends in a small rock room full of gold. I don't know why my grandfather dug the tunnel so far out. The rock that needs to be removed is massive, but doesn't stretch all the way to O'Mally's..." He stilled his babbling tongue. "Needless to say, the tunnel is very narrow and tight. A man barely has enough room to move or breathe in it."

"And you're claustrophobic, right?" Bethany asked, reading Edwin's eyes.

"Yes," Edwin admitted miserably. "Greg Cranmore was also claustrophobic. Brian Amerson took a camera and explored the tunnel, filming everything. He assured me there was tons of gold waiting to be dug up." Edwin narrowed his twitching eyes. "I allowed Brian to use some of the gold he brought out of the tunnel to buy part of my grandfather's land."

"Why did you wait instead of mining the gold?" Bethany

asked.

Edwin hungered to strangle Bethany to death. "My grandfather is—was—an old man. I was due to inherit everything he owned. I didn't want to upset him or make him angry at me. If I did, the old man might have taken me out of his will. It was better to wait...only, the old man kept on living. I'm not getting any younger. Can you understand that?"

"I can't understand why you killed Greg Cranmore and Brian Amerson," Bethany confessed. "It seems to me you needed them—Greg Cranmore to conduct your real estate translations and Brian Amerson to dig out your gold."

"Are you stupid?" Edwin snapped. "Greg Cranmore was going to stick a knife in my back. Brian Amerson had no intention of letting me live, either. Every man had his own plan. Live or die, the last man living gets the gold, right? But I outsmarted my enemies. They couldn't touch the gold as long as I was alive."

"Why?"

"Because I exhausted myself inserting hidden cameras into that awful tunnel my grandfather dug. If anyone entered the tunnel, the hidden cameras would alert me and I would detonate a series of explosives that I'd planted. While it's true I am claustrophobic, I forced myself to carry out a series of desperate measures." He looked up at Bethany. "I was waiting for my grandfather to die, but when I realized the old man was going to keep on living, I knew the time to act had come. When you showed up in town, I saw my scapegoat. After all, didn't you write a book about the perfect murder, Ms. Lights?"

"You're a monster," Bethany, sickened, told Edwin. "You have no regard for human life. You simply hunger for power, money, and control. You're a soulless creature destined for a very horrible nightmare that will soon become your eternity. A nightmare that will hold you captive forever."

"I'm an atheist," Edwin nearly spat at Bethany, feeling a strange anger replace his fear. An anger that felt cursed. "I believe that when a person dies, that's it. Nothing exists after life."

"You're going to find out your belief is a lie," Bethany promised Edwin in a voice that shattered the man's anger. Edwin felt his heart drop into the mouth of a dark, hungry abyss.

Bethany drew in a very deep breath and called out in a loud voice: "Snowman...snowman...snowman..."

"That's my cue!" Henry bolted to his feet before Edwin knew what was happening. "Hands in the air now!" he yelled in a rough cop's voice while aiming his gun directly at Edwin. "Hands in the air! You got three seconds, boy. Hands in the air!"

"What..." Edwin stumbled off the stool he was sitting on and hit the floor. Henry flew around the counter before he could blink. "A cop?! What is this?!"

"Hands in the air!" Henry yelled again. Without any warning, he fired off a single bullet that struck the floor, landing a mere inch from Edwin's head. Edwin let out a horrible cry and threw his hands into the air.

"Roll over onto your stomach and keep your hands where I can see them. Bethany, cover me while I handcuff this rat. If he moves, shoot him."

Bethany rushed out from behind the counter and covered Henry while the man bravely slapped a pair of handcuffs onto Edwin. Once the handcuffs were secure, Henry snatched Edwin to his feet, then fished out a priceless tape recorder. He handed the tape recorder to Bethany. Bethany hit the stop button.

"Mr. McCrandy, I didn't know Greg Cranmore very well or Brian Amerson," she said. "I can't say I'll lose any sleep over the death of those two men. But you did kill an innocent old man who lived a full life and most likely had a few good years left to live. You show no remorse. I wish I could make you feel remorse, but I can't. Instead, I'm going to give your grandfather a gift."

"What are you talking about?" Edwin nearly screamed his head off.

Bethany turned to the front counter, picked up a lone cinnamon bun, and swung back around to face Edwin. "This," she stated. Edwin watched with shocked eyes as Bethany took a bite of the cinnamon bun.

"But...that cinnamon bun..." Edwin stuttered in shock.

"The camera sitting in the far corner is a dummy camera, too," Bethany informed Edwin as she chewed the cinnamon bun. "I never recorded my interaction with Brian Amerson. No one is watching us. I simply outsmarted you. And I do pray your grandfather will take joy in that fact somehow. Rest his soul."

Edwin watched Bethany polish off the cinnamon bun. "I'll kill you! Someday! Mark my word!"

"Boy," Henry told Edwin, "the only place you're going is prison." He pointed at the tape recorder Bethany was holding. "You dug your own grave."

He grinned at Bethany. "Not bad. Remind me to never get on your bad side."

Bethany wanted to hug Henry, but knew he had a job to do. "Mind if I walk down to the police station with you? I'm sure Detective Spencer and Andrew are going to have a lot of questions. I hope they won't be too upset with me."

"Bethany, in Snow Falls, it doesn't matter how a killer is caught, just as long as the job gets done." Henry grabbed Edwin's right arm. "Move," he ordered. Before Edwin could take a step, a sleepy raccoon ran out from behind the counter and peed on his leg.

Well, that's a perfect ending to a miserable killer, Bethany thought as she glanced around the front room of her coffee shop. *Now maybe I can finally begin my life...I pray I can.*

chapter nine

Sarah smiled the perfect smile. Even though Bethany and Henry had taken a very dangerous risk, they had captured a hungry killer. Bethany had set a clever trap and bluffed a prowling wolf. What courage—and heart.

"I'm so proud of you, Bethany," Sarah told Bethany in a loving voice. "You are an amazing woman."

Bethany blushed. She knew Sarah was being kind; yet, her heart didn't know how to accept a sincere compliment. *It's going to take time to heal,* she reminded herself as she took a much-needed sip of coffee. *You spent twenty-one years being abused by a cruel man. You're not going to let down your defenses overnight. It's going to take time. And now I have all the time I need.*

"I'm just grateful Edwin McCrandy is behind bars."

"I'm grateful I still have a job," Henry pointed out. He glanced worriedly at Andrew, who was sitting on the edge of a vacant desk, staring at him. "Right, boss?"

Andrew let out a heavy sigh. "Henry, you know your job is secure. You're the best cop in town, but I swear, if you ever do something so crazy again, I'll feed you to the first grizzly bear I can find."

"I second that," Conrad added. He locked eyes with

Bethany. "What you did was very stupid. You could have gotten yourself killed—and Henry killed. You are not a trained cop. Watching silly television shows like *Murder, She Wrote* does not qualify a person to become a homicide detective." He kept his voice stern. "You didn't know the mindset of Edwin McCrandy, how he might have reacted, who he might have hurt."

Sarah held up her right hand. "I think Bethany understands," she told Conrad.

"It's alright, Sarah. I understand Detective Spencer's anger. I did take a dangerous chance," Bethany said calmly. "It's his job to lecture me."

Something in Bethany's eyes—a certain look—caused Conrad to back off. His intention was to scold Bethany a little, not upset the poor woman.

"Well...what's done is done," he said. "And from what Henry told me, you did a good job. I'm not upset with you. Actually, from what Henry explained and from what I heard on the tape recorder, you did a great job. I'm impressed. You remind me a lot of my wife. She's hard-headed, too."

"I'll remember you said that when it's time to cook dinner," Sarah teased Conrad, grateful her husband had backed down.

"I mean it," Conrad softened his tone. "Bethany, you did take a dangerous chance, but from a cop's point of view, you did an excellent job bluffing a killer. I'm proud of you and Henry. As angry as I want to be, the truth is, there's no telling how many lives you and Henry saved. A monster like Edwin McCrandy would have continued to kill. I'm certain of that."

"Thank you, Detective Spencer." Bethany managed a grateful smile.

"My name is Conrad," Conrad smiled back. "My wife has other choice names for me, but you can call me Conrad."

Bethany laughed, relief flooding her heart. Conrad wasn't such a bad guy. He was a tough New York cop, but deep down, the guy had a soft heart. "Well, if it's alright, I think I'll have someone take me home. I still have a great deal of unpacking to do, and I desperately want a hot shower and a soft bed."

"I second that." Henry fought back a yawn. "Andy should be here in a few minutes, Andrew. Be alright if I check out for the day and go on home?"

"Sure, Henry. And thanks." Andrew stood up and shook Henry's hand. "Snow Falls couldn't survive without you."

"Tell that to my wife whenever I want a pot roast dinner," Henry smiled. "See you tomorrow. I'm working the eight-to-four shift."

"See you then." Andrew walked Henry to the front door and saw his friend off. "Drive safe!"

"Come on, honey. Conrad and I will drive you to your cabin since the battery on your truck is dead. We'll pick you up tomorrow and get you a new battery." Sarah handed Bethany her coat. "Andrew, you go home and get some sleep when Fred arrives."

Andrew tossed a thumb back toward a short hallway that led to a room holding three iron cells. "Fred is going to have a boring shift. Snow Falls is once again safe."

Sarah helped Bethany put her coat on. "Thanks to Bethany's daring mind," she pointed out, hugging Bethany's shoulder. "People in Snow Falls will understand that you are a fighter, Bethany. In this town, that's a good notch to have on your belt."

Conrad looked into Bethany's eyes. The poor woman was exhausted. It was time to call it a day. "Come on, let's get moving. The snow is coming down heavy again. I want to get home, get a hot shower, have a warm meal, and spend the evening with my daughter. Andrew, see you tomorrow. I'll write up my report then."

"There's no rush, Conrad. We have another storm front moving in that's going to dump at least another two feet of snow on us. It's going to be a while before the state police can come and take Edwin McCrandy off our hands. Three or four days at the least." Andrew urged back a yawn. "Go on home and be with Little Sarah. Give that sweet baby a kiss from her Uncle Andrew."

"Will do." Andrew took Sarah's hand. "Let's go, honey."

Sarah nodded. "Bye, Andrew," she called out, then hurried out into the heavy snow with Conrad and Bethany at her side. "The sun is getting ready to set. Temperature is dropping very fast and winds are rough again. It's going to be a stormy night," she spoke over a howling wind, looking around at a sleepy little town full of glowing windows that were going out one by one. "Everyone's getting ready to go home."

Bethany stood very still as her eyes soaked in a beautiful winter wonderland. Snow Falls was a small town. The main street consisted of a police station, a diner, and two empty stores scarred by countless hard winters. Cozy neighborhoods surrounded the main street; streets with small but welcoming cabins that reminded Bethany of little gingerbread homes. The business district stood five miles northeast of the downtown area—well, if you could call a few restaurants, two gas stations, a hotel, a garage, and O'Mally's department store a business district.

The library is south of town, sitting next to the Snow Falls river. The elementary, middle, and high schools are off to my west...small schools that still belong in the 1950s. And numerous cabins are peppered around the county. That's all. There's nothing else to Snow Falls. This little town is a world of its own. The closet town is fifty miles south of us. A person truly is alone this far up...and that's just the way I like it.

"What are you thinking?"

"Huh?" Sarah's warm voice caught Bethany off-guard.

Sarah put her arm around Bethany, ignoring the falling

snow and icy winds. "You became lost in thought. What were you thinking?"

Bethany continued to look around. Her weary eyes traveled to the Snow Falls Bakery. "I was thinking about redemption," she spoke over the wind. "Snow Falls is a small town, Sarah. There's nothing here, really...yet, everything I need to feel content is in Snow Falls." Bethany kept her eyes on the glowing windows of the bakery. "I feel so lost at times, like Ebenezer Scrooge after he began his journey through a life that consisted of many thorns and a great deal of pain and anger that formed him into a cold soul."

"I see how lost you feel when I look into your eyes," Sarah told Bethany, then asked Conrad to pull his truck around. "Bethany and I need to talk."

Conrad nodded and started off down a snow-soaked sidewalk. He had parked his truck behind the police station. No big deal. Sarah needed time to talk to Bethany. A man knew when to take a walk.

"I wish I could tell you life gets easier," Sarah spoke to Bethany, forcing her voice to rise above the screaming winds.

"That's a very good line," Bethany sighed, daring to keep her head up instead of bowing down to the icy winds. She touched the front of her coat with a gloved hand. "The memories will always remain in here—the heart. I can't escape that prison. But there is hope...and beauty in hope." She finally turned to face Sarah as hard snow struck her beautiful face. "Sarah, I know I took a dangerous risk, but I had to. Before you ask why, I think you know why."

"I think I do," Sarah nodded, ignoring the snow. "You're tired of being scared."

"I'm tired of being bullied, yes," Bethany admitted. "I moved to Snow Falls to start a new life. I didn't move to Snow Falls to be bullied or to constantly be afraid, or to be kicked down like a dog. All I kept seeing was my husband's eyes—those awful eyes

—sneering at me, calling me ugly names, tearing me down, beating me down with cruel words. It was as if my husband had come back to life somehow, determined to destroy all my hopes and dreams." Bethany felt tears begin to slip from her eyes. "I had to fight, please understand that. I couldn't simply run scared anymore. Oh, it's all so confusing! I feel like I'm tied into a million knots!" She threw her arms up into the snow. "Why didn't I simply run? Why did I take such a dangerous, irresponsible, impractical chance? Why didn't I go home to North Carolina and let my mother dictate the rest of my life?"

"Because you're a grown woman, Bethany," Sarah spoke in a gentle, patient voice. "You're also a woman who is desperate to start healing from a broken past." She looked around at the white blanket of snow covering the downtown area. "Bethany, you went after Edwin McCrandy because you decided to fight instead of cower. That tells me that deep down, inside your heart, you are ready to start healing. You're ready to fight. You're ready to prove to the world that you can endure another round. While it's true your life is not going to get any easier, at least you can hold onto the truth that your life will start to heal...and you know what?"

"What?"

Sarah wiped Bethany's tears. "You aren't alone. You have me and Amanda...and if Amanda's cousin decides to stay in Snow Falls, who knows? Maybe the two of you might become best friends." She put her arm around Bethany. "You remind me a lot of myself. When I moved to Snow Falls, I was a very broken woman. I never dreamed it was possible that I would fall in love again, trust again, let alone have a daughter. I had to fight my way through many nightmares, but here I am. And Bethany, in the end, you're going to be alright, too."

"In the end?" Bethany asked. "Why can't the happy ending be now?"

Sarah touched Bethany's heart. "Because there is a war

going on inside you. When you win the war, the happy ending will open a bright doorway for you to enter."

Bethany glanced back at the Snow Falls Bakery. *Scrooge...Scrooge...*she heard Jacob Marley's creepy voice howl. *Scrooge...there is no chance to ever be redeemed...you're hopeless...* Then she heard Jacob call out her own name. *Bethany...there is no hope for you...you can never be redeemed. You're too broken...you can't win.* "I want to go home, Sarah." She forced her eyes away from the bakery's glowing window. "I'm very tired."

"I understand, but before Conrad pulls around, can I ask you one question?" Sarah asked. Bethany offered a weak nod. "In your book, you did create the perfect murder. I spent most of last night reading your book online. I was very impressed at how well you wrote the book. The murder was brilliant."

"Sarah, I regret every word I wrote—"

"Don't," Sarah insisted. "What I saw in each word I read was a very hurt and angry woman who needed to vent her emotions. Writing is a great way to do that. I guess what I'm saying, or what I want to ask you is, do you think that perhaps writing a second book might be good for you?"

Bethany stared at Sarah in shock as tears rolled down her frozen red cheeks. "Another book? I despise the first book I wrote. I can't believe I even allowed myself to write such an awful book. I'm a children's author, Sarah, not a killer."

"Of course, you're not a killer," Sarah assured Bethany, starting to feel the icy cold winds snapping at her body heat. "I'm simply suggesting that writing can be a healthy venue." She touched Bethany's heart again. "The more you try to keep the war bottled up, the more you're going to struggle to have peace. Think about that."

"But writing a second book? Wouldn't that turn me into a monster? Make me no better than Edwin McCrandy?" Bethany cried.

"No," Sarah said simply. "You're not a monster, Bethany. And there is nothing wrong with releasing years of hurt and years of anger into words. I should know—I still write books myself, and I find my past still leaks out in some of the words I write."

Before Bethany could speak, Conrad pulled his truck around. The plow attached to the front of his truck was at the ready, prepared to fight the snow. "Is this the start of a nightmare or a peaceful dream?" she whispered to herself as Conrad pulled his truck up. *As much as I want to insist the nightmare is over, something deep in my heart is telling me the nightmare I tried to escape from is just beginning for me. Maybe that's why Sarah is suggesting I write a second book. There is a war taking place inside me. Writing has always been my escape, but right now, I'm simply too tired to think anymore. Christmas is on the way. I'll just rest until after Christmas is over and step onto the battlefield again.*

A set of murderous eyes watched Sarah walk Bethany to Conrad's truck. Bethany gratefully climbed into the cab of the truck and vanished.

"I'll let you relax, and then I'll kill you," Tara Sterling spoke as Conrad pulled away from the police station, plowing the snow as he did. "My mother is dead and it's all your fault. You're going to suffer for what you did. I'm going to make you suffer...in time. But first, I want you to feel safe before I kill you."

Tara slipped back into a frozen alley, attached her feet to a pair of skis, then quickly vanished into the snow.

chapter ten

"I can't believe Christmas is in one week," Bethany told Julie as she kicked snow off a pair of white winter boots. "Downtown Snow Falls looks so beautiful with all the Christmas lights put up, and just look at O'Mally's. Sarah and Amanda have the inside of the store looking like a Christmas wonderland."

Julie Walsh took in the warm, beautifully Christmas-themed department store that brought peace and happiness to her heart. Cozy Christmas music drifted down from overhead speakers, catching a ride on a Christmas train that ran a route about three feet under the ceiling, looping around the entire department store through snow-covered tunnels, bridges, and little towns. Christmas trees stood everywhere, decorated with old-fashioned 1970 lights, tinsel, and ornaments. Life-sized presents covered with red and green wrapping paper nestled up against little forest creatures standing in front of smiling snowmen holding candy canes. The entire department store resembled a giant Christmas paradise that warmed everyone's hearts.

"It is very lovely in here," Julie's British accent rang out as she removed a blue snow cap. Snow dropped off the cap and struck her dark brown coat.

Bethany pulled off a green ski hat that matched her lovely green coat that was quickly becoming worn in. "I especially love how the snack café resembles Grandma's kitchen. All those cakes and cookies and pies, and all the employees are dressed like carolers. It's all so cozy. Sarah and Amanda did a remarkable job."

"Quit talking and start shopping!"

"What?" Bethany turned around and spotted Amanda walking up to them. She was wearing a red and green dress and a red and white stocking cap.

"Everything is twenty percent off except the toilet paper and paper towels." Amanda offered Bethany and Julie a quick hug. "The store is crowded, so you might have to fight your way through the crowds," she teased.

Bethany smelled a chili dog on Amanda's breath. She smiled. "Been at the snack café again?"

"You bet I have," Amanda beamed. "I had myself three chili dogs, some chili cheese fries, a pretzel, and a hot coffee… and that's just to hold me over until lunch."

"She's eating us out of house and home."

Bethany turned and spotted Sarah approaching. Sarah was dressed identical to Amanda, yet, somehow, Amanda seemed a bit cheerier. "The store looks amazing."

"Thanks, honey." Sarah eyed Amanda in a way that made Amanda wince. "Stephanie told me we're running low on kosher hot dogs again and our delivery isn't until Monday. Stephanie also told me she's missing a few boxes of the chocolate candy canes we ordered. Mind if I smell your breath?"

"Well, a gal has to fill her tummy, love," Amanda whimpered, then scurried behind Julie. "Save me, cousin."

Sarah threw her hands up into the air. "Amanda, you're eating us out of house and home. What am I going to do with you?"

"Go get me a second plate of chili fries?" Amanda suggested.

Sarah looked at Amanda in a way that made everyone wince. "May I suggest you go help Amy? She needs assistance in the toy aisle. Mark called in sick, and so did Gennifer and Paula. Brad can't make it in because he's grounded for throwing snowballs at Old Man Mills. We're short-handed, and as you can see, we have a full house, so may I suggest you focus on work instead of your tummy, business partner?"

"Boy, are you grumpy," Amanda told Sarah, and then scuttled behind Bethany. "Don't let her kill me."

"I'm not grumpy. It's just that the food is for the customers and...oh, what's the point?" Sarah dropped her head. "Amanda, what am I going to do with you?"

"Go get me another chili dog?"

Sarah simply let out a defeated laugh. "Maybe later, but right now, Amy does need help. I'll be in women's clothing helping Susan." Sarah reached out and patted Bethany's shoulder. "You and Julie shop until you drop. The shopping carts are over there." She pointed to a row of red and green shopping carts and hurried away.

"I'll be in toys," Amanda said, giggling and dancing away to the sounds of Bing Crosby.

"Those two are a riot," Julie smiled.

"Best friends for life," Bethany agreed.

"Sisters for life," Julie corrected Bethany. "I'm jealous of them. I've never had a real friend."

"Never?" Bethany asked, walking Julie over to the shopping carts.

"Acquaintances, mostly. I was never tidy when it came to the night club scene. I preferred quiet evenings at home. My husband preferred to participate in the night club scene." Julie retrieved a shopping cart. "Ben is a lawyer. A brilliant lawyer, to be quite honest. But he is a chap who has a wild heart to him. When we first met, I had a wild heart, too. But after my son was born, I settled down. When my son turned two years old, I found Jesus Christ and accepted Him as my Lord and Savior. I tried to get Ben to attend church but managed to turn him into my enemy instead. So," Julie drew in a sad breath, "for the next sixteen years, my husband tolerated me and my beliefs while he lived his life and I lived mine. During the last three years of our marriage, he managed to turn my son against me."

"I'm so sorry, Julie." Bethany felt relieved Julie was opening up to her. After Edwin McCrandy was arrested, things had settled down. Sarah and Amanda made sure to constantly keep Bethany in their sights, inviting her over for dinner or helping her out however they could. But the time arrived when Sarah and Amanda had to focus entirely on O'Mally's. They managed to have Julie start spending time with Bethany. Julie was happy to oblige, but still remained distant. Now the woman was finally opening up to her new friend, which was a welcoming sign. "It certainly seems like you and I have a great deal in common."

"Yes, it does," Julie agreed. She had to admit she felt a special bond toward Bethany. Bethany was a broken woman, just like she was—but there was a deeper bond, a mystery she couldn't explain. She simply felt as if she had known Bethany all her life, the way sisters know one another. The feeling was strange. "Maybe one night we can eat chocolate and complain about our ex-husbands."

"Well, my husband is dead, but I still have some complaints." Bethany managed to smile. "Sarah suggested I write a second book as a form of therapy, I suppose." She removed her coat, revealing a dark green sweater. She placed her coat in the shopping cart Julie had retrieved. "When I wrote my first book, I felt hideous, in a sense. I was consumed with a great deal of anger and pain. In my book, I killed off my husband. I felt very awful afterward, but now I'm beginning to realize I was simply venting my emotions...trying to find peace. I really didn't kill my husband. I was simply trying to kill the pain my husband was inflicting on me."

Julie nodded and began to make her way toward the snack café as Bing Crosby sang about walking in a winter wonderland. "Writing is good therapy. I used to keep a diary. I stopped a few years back, though. I wish I had the ability to write books. I can barely write a full page without losing track of my thoughts."

"What kind of work did you do in London?"

"I worked as a cook in a hotel," Julie explained. "I love to cook, but don't tell Cousin Amanda. Cousin Amanda hasn't asked about my past. She's been so kind letting me stay with her, and well...we haven't talked about the past very much." Julie stopped at the entrance to the snack café and parked the shopping cart. "My mother was British, but my father was American. I was born in Nashville, Tennessee. When I was three months old, my mother begged my father to take her back to London, so I grew up in London and attended a very posh cooking school there."

"Sounds fun."

Julie studied the snack café. She spotted a group of old men sitting at a booth, sipping on hot coffees. She noticed each man had a woman's coat sitting on his lap. She smiled. Old men watching their wives' coats. Some things never changed. "It was...for a while. I enjoyed the night life, but when my son was born, something changed inside my heart. I began craving the simple things in life. So I quit my job at the hotel, started a small catering business, and began working out of my kitchen, but my business didn't find success. My heart was more into being a mother."

Bethany walked Julie up to the front counter of the snack café. A pretty red-headed girl was standing behind the counter, making a pot of fresh coffee. Bethany politely ordered two coffees and two salty pretzels. "My treat," she smiled.

"Thank you, but I have money. I didn't let my ex-husband leave me penniless. As you Americans say, I took him to the bank." A deep frown came over Julie's face. "I suppose that's one of the reasons my son refuses to speak to me. He blames me for forcing his father to leave our home and move into a crummy flat."

Bethany looked into Julie's eyes, seeing a great deal of pain there. *I'm not the only one who is hurting or broken. Julie, bless her sweet soul, is just as hurt and broken as I am. Maybe that's one of the reasons we're connecting so well.* "My treat," Bethany insisted in a sweet voice.

Julie smiled. "I'll go find us a booth. It'll be nice to sit, have coffee, and relax. I have been on edge lately." She looked around, a hope entering her heart. "Who knows, Bethany. Maybe someday, God might send two good men who will truly love us?"

"I don't think I'm ready to even entertain that idea," Bethany managed to laugh.

Julie laughed back and wandered away to find a booth. As she did, a young, beautiful—breathtakingly beautiful—black-headed girl stepped into the snack café. She had the silkiest black hair Bethany had ever seen in her life.

My, she's a lovely young lady. She looks to be half-Asian, too. Asian women are always so lovely and graceful. I'm always so flat and bland.

Tara Sterling approached Bethany, wearing a casual expression as she talked on a gray cell phone. "Yes, Mom, I know...but you know how grandfather is...I'll buy him a tie and some winter gloves and he'll be happy...alright, I'll call you later. Bye." She stuffed the cell phone she was holding into the pocket of a white coat that brought out every feature of her chiseled beauty. "My mother and I decided to visit my grandfather for Christmas this year," she told Bethany without preamble, not seeming concerned she was speaking to a stranger. "This is the first year without my grandmother."

"Oh, I'm sorry."

Tara shrugged her shoulders. "I'm twenty-five, my mother is fifty-four, and my grandfather is pushing eighty-five. Can't stop the aging process…and with age, comes death. That's the cycle of life."

Bethany wasn't sure how to respond to Tara's blunt statement. "Well, yes, unfortunately that's true."

"Give me a coffee and a cheeseburger, ketchup and cheese only," Tara called out to the girl working behind the snack counter. She began digging into her blue and white purse. Seconds later, her right hand pulled out a bottle of pills. Bethany watched as Tara opened the pill bottle and downed two pills. "I get bad headaches. All this Christmas shopping isn't helping."

"Oh, I'm sorry to hear that. Headaches are very awful." Bethany's eyes flickered to Julie. Her friend was now in a warm booth, looking around at all the cozy decorations.

"Your order is ready, ma'am," the girl behind the snack counter called out to Bethany. "Will you be paying with cash or card?"

"Uh, cash." Bethany whipped out a ten-dollar bill from a brown purse. She handed the money to the girl, then picked up a wooden tray holding two coffees and two salty pretzels. "Keep the change, honey," she said and walked away, leaving Tara standing alone. As far as Bethany was concerned, Tara was just another face, some young girl who carried a hard attitude that wasn't very appealing. *The world still has good people in it, though,* Bethany reminded herself as she carefully moved toward Julie.

Tara sourly watched Bethany join her friend. She waited for her order, then sat in a booth close to Bethany and Julie. She ate in silence, then departed the snack café without saying a word, finding her way back to the toy aisle.

"Can I help you find anything, love?" Amanda asked Tara as she entered the aisle. She was stocking a new shipment of toys on aisle three.

"Just browsing."

Amanda looked at Tara. "Are you new in town, love? I've never seen you before."

"I'm visiting my grandfather," Tara answered in a cold tone that made Amanda shrug her shoulders and return to work without asking more questions.

Tara whipped out her cell phone again and pretended to make a call. "It's me...yes, Mom, I'm still doing my shopping...I'm standing in some lame toy aisle...Mom, I'm twenty-five years old, single, and standing in a lame department store in Alaska, do you really expect me to be happy? Yes...I know...listen, what was I supposed to get Timmy...stupid toys...yes, I'll try to simmer down my attitude...bye." Tara turned to Amanda. "Where are the footballs?"

"Aisle five," Amanda answered.

Tara nodded and moved away.

"What a bitter spider that one is," Amanda mumbled under her breath, not realizing Tara had set her up.

Tara eventually found Sarah and conducted another fake call. When she ended the call, she threw an ugly sweater into a shopping cart and wandered away. Sarah watched Tara make her way toward the front checkout lines. Seeing a strange face in Snow Falls at Christmastime wasn't anything out of the ordinary, so Sarah shrugged her shoulders and went back to helping her colleague unpack a new shipment of sweaters.

Tara casually checked out and left O'Mally's. She walked to her green Jeep, making her way through a heavy falling snow.

"Phase one complete," she said to herself with a grin. "I'll visit Bethany's coffee shop tomorrow, and when she least expects it—when anyone least expects it—I'll strike. Only I've had a change of plans...instead of just killing Bethany, I'm going to kill all her friends first and really make her suffer. Bethany thinks she was so smart by outsmarting some lame killer. She's in for a very rude surprise this time. I'll also get my money. My plan is working perfectly!"

"You're always sleeping," Bethany fussed at Rascal. Rascal was the name she had given to her raccoon friend. "Eating and sleeping. Good grief."

She pushed a broom past the doggy bed Rascal was sleeping on and continued to the back of the front counter. "Maybe we'll get a customer today? The snow has let up and the front street is plowed."

Soft Christmas music danced out of an old record player Bethany had set on the front counter. Perry Como was singing about Toyland, a song Bethany adored. She imagined herself living in a winter-themed Toyland on a faraway arctic island filled with beautiful toys that could laugh and talk and sing. *I'm always dreaming of being so very far away. Snow Falls is my Toyland for now. Maybe in Heaven, I'll have a real Toyland?* She continued to sweep, becoming lost in her thoughts. She didn't notice when the front door to the coffee shop opened.

"Are you open?"

Bethany lifted her head and spotted a familiar face. It was the young lady from O'Mally's she had seen the day before. "Yes, I'm open," she called out, feeling at ease. After all, Edwin McCrandy was now being held in Anchorage. The killer was far away from Snow Falls. Bethany seriously doubted if there were any more killers lurking about in the snow. "Please, come in."

Tara watched Bethany put down her broom and wipe her hands on a yellow and green apron that was covering a silly

Christmas-themed dress. She closed the front door and kicked snow off her boots. "It's warm in here," she said casually. "I'm from West Palm Beach, Florida. I'm not used to the cold."

Bethany didn't detect an accent in the young woman's voice. *She's dressed like someone who is spoiled and rich. That white leather coat she's wearing looks like it cost a fortune. And that fur hat surely wasn't picked up in a thrift store.* "Well, Alaska without the cold and snow would be like having no sand or sunshine in Florida."

"True," Tara nodded. She worked her way up to the front counter and took a seat on a middle stool. "Let's see," she said, raising her eyes up to a friendly chalkboard. "I think I'll have a regular coffee and a coffee donut."

"I'm not set up to take credit cards yet. I can only accept cash."

"I have cash," Tara assured.

Bethany forced a smile to her lips. "Even if you didn't, coffee is on the house. It is Christmas, after all." With those words, Bethany set out to fill Tara's order.

Tara waited. But as soon as Bethany approached her, carrying a coffee cup, she forced her face into a bored but friendly expression. "Nice place you have. I like all the decorations. A little corny, but not too bad."

Bethany set down Tara's cup of coffee and pointed to a glass jar that held packets of powder creamer and sugar. "Don't you like Christmas?"

"Christmas has become too commercialized for me," Tara answered. She removed her white gloves and went for the glass jar. "Besides, Christmas has nothing to do with the Bible."

"Well, it's true that Jesus probably wasn't born in December. And I admit that Santa Claus has nothing to do with the birth of our Savior. I'm aware that the feast of God points to our Savior's true birth." Bethany watched Tara open a packet of creamer. "Christmastime, to me, represents a time of year where families can come together, love each other, forgive offenses, and share in the warmth of tenderness and joy."

"And make the merchants rich, right?" Tara asked sarcastically.

"Well, I admit that buying a dead tree while cleaning out our bank accounts isn't exactly wise. That's why I own a plastic tree and set a limit on how much I spend at Christmas each year." *My, is this young lady bitter. How old did she say she was? Oh yes, twenty-five.* "Let me get you a donut." Bethany retrieved a green and red paper plate from the back counter and pulled out a donut from a glass pastry case. "Here you go."

Tara accepted her donut with a quick hand. "I'd rather be back in Florida. I'm an actress. I perform in a lot of high-profile plays. I had to skip out in performing my role as the wife of George Bailey this year." Tara snagged a sugar packet. "My mother insisted I take this trip with her."

This young woman seems like a spoiled brat to me. Oh well, a customer is a customer. Besides, it was getting a bit lonely. Julie is helping Sarah and Amanda at O'Mally's. Conrad and Andrew are busy. Henry has a cold, bless his heart. It's just been me and Rascal all morning. "I'm new to Snow Falls myself. I don't know many people. Uh...who is your grandfather?"

"A grumpy, rude old man," Tara cleverly answered without giving any name. "A grumpy, rude old man who pretends he likes me. The guy smells like old pipe tobacco. Lame."

"Well, it's not easy being old. You need to be patient." Bethany felt her desire for company quickly fading. The young lady sitting in her coffee shop needed to take a quick walk outside.

"Yeah, that's what my mother tells me." Tara nodded as she poured another packet of sugar into her coffee. "I guess I'm upset because I missed out on playing my usual

Christmas role. A lot of important people visit the theater I perform at." She grabbed a red coffee straw and began stirring her coffee. "Well, what's your story? Why did you move to this one-horse town?"

"I decided it was time for me to begin a new life after my husband was killed in a car accident," Bethany answered cautiously.

"Whose idea was it to give some sixteen-year-old brat a driver's license?" Tara huffed instead of showing compassion. "We're so stupid. We drive down roads at dangerous speeds with only a line of paint separating us from being smashed into pieces. If there are aliens out in the universe, I'm sure they look down at us humans and roll their eyes."

"Well, the human race has marched forward as far as technology is concerned...but morally, ethically, and spiritually, I believe the human race has declined. It's no surprise that we take such dangerous risks with our lives on a daily basis when people barely care about each other," Bethany said. *This young lady is making me lose my Christmas happiness...not that I had much happiness to begin with.* "Well, I'll be in the kitchen if you need me."

"Sure."

Bethany glanced down and spotted the hidden Glock 19 sitting under the front counter. *I doubt I'll need my gun today. Maybe a can of attitude-changer.* She made her way to the kitchen, leaving the young woman alone.

Tara quickly scanned the front room. There were no windows present. A heavy door separated the back kitchen from the front room. For the time being, she was absolutely alone.

Without wasting a second, she took out her cell phone and began filming the interior of the front room. "Perfect," she grinned. "I'm filming your grave, Bethany."

After filming the front room, Tara put her cell phone away and returned to sipping her hot cup of coffee. She nibbled on her donut until Bethany reappeared, carrying a freshly baked tray of cinnamon buns that were most likely going to end up in Amanda's tummy. "Smells good," Tara complimented.

"Would you like one on the house?" Bethany offered, setting the tray down on the front counter.

"Not me. I'm watching every calorie I eat. This donut is a real no-no, and so is the creamer and sugar I put into my coffee. I'm going to have to do a thousand crunches before bed." Tara dropped the donut she was holding. "I think I bumped into you yesterday at the department store, right?"

"I believe so. Briefly, yes," Bethany nodded.

"I saw you sitting with a friend. Must be nice to have a friend. I don't have any friends," Tara said, allowing her voice to become tinged with sadness. "Most people think I'm too sarcastic or standoffish. The truth is, I have a hard time making friends. Trust is a real big issue with me."

"I believe trust is an issue with most people." Bethany wiped her hands on her apron. "Sometimes we have to reach out and be a friend in order to make a friend."

"That's easy for you to say. You're not an aspiring actress who's been stabbed in the back by all her friends just to land some lousy role in a stupid play." Tara snatched up her coffee again. "I'm part Asian. Some of my...ex-friends...send me rude messages on my social media account. Why? Because I always play the wife of George Bailey. I suppose I can only play the part if I'm not half-Asian, right?"

"Some people can be very rude." *Whew, Snow Falls certainly attracts the bitter and broken-hearted, that's for certain.* "I'm sure in time—"

"In time?" Tara rolled her eyes. "Do you know what I'm doing on Christmas Eve?"

Bethany shook her head no.

"My mother and grandfather are going over to some old lady's cabin. I'm being left alone to watch corny old movies and drink eggnog. Story of my life."

"Don't you have a boyfriend? You're very pretty and—"

"I don't date guys who look at me because I'm pretty on the outside. I'm waiting to meet a guy who sees me for who I am on the inside. Besides, most of the guys I know are lame. Real losers who think they're going to be the next Val Kilmer or something."

"I'm sorry. I didn't mean to pry."

"Oh, it's no big deal." Tara let her voice relax. "So, what are you doing on Christmas Eve?" she asked, taking another sip of coffee. "Eating lame turkey sandwiches?"

"I'm having a small gathering right here in my coffee shop the night before Christmas Eve," Bethany replied. "One of my friends has a son who's going to visit on Christmas Eve. Another friend will be spending Christmas Eve at the police station with her husband and daughter—her husband is a detective. My other friend will be spending Christmas Eve with her cousin, the friend who has the visiting son." *Boy, that was a mouthful. Never thought I'd be explaining what my friends would be doing on Christmas Eve. Like this young lady, I've never had any real friends before.*

"Sounds cool," Tara said. "All your friends snuggled up in this warm little coffee shop."

"Well, not all. Just Sarah, Amanda, and Julie," Bethany explained, naming her friends. And why not? The young lady sitting before her wasn't a threat. "Sarah's husband has to work and Amanda's husband hurt his right ankle."

"Hey, an all-ladies night. Even better, right?" Tara beamed. "You can eat chocolate until you throw up and sing lousy songs. Sounds like a good time." She took another sip of her coffee. "If you want an extra leg, call me. I wouldn't mind hanging out for a while and getting fat on chocolate. Of course I'd have to do a million crunches."

"Well...the coffee shop will be closed, but..." Bethany stared into Tara's face. The young woman appeared to be so...lonely. "You're more than welcome to come to the party.

We're going to have pizza, play a few games, and exchange presents."

"I wouldn't want to be a third wheel, but it would sure beat sitting in my grandfather's stuffy old cabin, getting fat on eggnog." Tara pretended to consider Bethany's offer. "Who would I buy a present for? I don't have much cash."

"Don't worry about buying a present." Bethany offered a kind smile. *Sarah and Amanda have been so kind to me, a complete stranger. How can I not be kind to this young lady at Christmas?* "The Christmas party begins at five. Bring some cookies."

"I can bring cookies," Tara smiled back—a smile that struck Bethany as strange-looking. "You're nice to invite me. Last year, I spent Christmas Eve alone, walking along the beach. It was lame."

I'm used to spending Christmas Eve alone. My husband was never home. "Well, this year you can spend Christmas Eve among friends," Bethany assured. "By the way, what's your name?"

"Tara Anderson," Tara lied. Tara had found an old man by the name of Curtis Anderson who lived alone in a cabin located ten miles northwest of town. He was currently suffering from dementia. The poor old man even believed Tara was his granddaughter. She had hacked into the Anderson's medical files while preparing her attack and found the perfect sap. "What's your name?"

"Bethany Lights," Bethany smiled. "It's nice to meet you, Tara."

"Likewise." Tara finished her coffee. "Can I have a refill? I'm in no rush to leave, and I'm definitely in no rush to go back to my grandfather's cabin and listen to him snore to death. And the smell...gross."

Bethany took Tara's cup and poured her more coffee. "Here you go."

"Great." Tara smiled her odd-looking smile again. Brilliant or not, a killer could never truly flash a genuine smile.

This young lady seems broken inside. I'm sure her smile reflects a hard life? Maybe all this young lady needs is a friend? "Well, since business is slow..." Bethany picked up a fresh cinnamon bun, said a prayer of thanks, and took a bite. "Care to chat some more?"

"Why not?" Tara shrugged. "You can tell me all about the Christmas party." She grinned inside her deadly heart. She had overheard Bethany telling Julie about the Christmas party. The party was going to allow Tara to kill Bethany's new friends while Bethany watched, and then kill Bethany...slowly and painfully. "It's like I said, I'm in no rush to go back to my grandfather's cabin and pull out my fingernails."

Bethany took another bite of her cinnamon bun and settled in for more chit-chat with her new friend.

As Bethany and Tara talked, a bored telephone sitting on Conrad's office desk rang. Conrad tossed a paper airplane into the air and answered the call, expecting the caller to be Sarah. "Detective Spencer speaking."

"Yes, this is Detective David Habersham. I'm down here in West Palm Beach, Florida."

"What can I do for you?" Conrad asked, leaning forward. Something in Detective Habersham's voice caused an alarm bell to go off inside his gut.

"I'm looking for a woman by the name of Tara Sterling," Detective Habersham explained. "She's wanted for questioning. Yesterday, I was given an alert. Tara used her bank card at a store called O'Mally's. She could be in your area or already gone."

"Send me a photo," Conrad ordered.

Detective Habersham assured Conrad he would fax over a photo ASAP—only the photo he faxed didn't resemble Tara at all. She had managed to completely alter her appearance. The photo Conrad received showed a woman who looked like a flimsy beach bum with blond hair. Tara's Asian features were barely noticeable in that photo.

For the time being, Tara Sterling was in the clear to strike...and to kill.

chapter eleven

Bethany didn't tell Sarah or Amanda about Tara until the morning of the Christmas party. O'Mally's had become a scene of hectic Christmas shopping. For a town the size of Snow Falls, residents had come out of the woodwork to get their shopping completed—or perhaps, Bethany thought as she stood with Sarah and Amanda inside a warm office, the residents of Snow Falls simply enjoyed a delightful department store that was, for once, decorated with love and joy.

Old Man O'Mally had never put much thought into decorations. A few lights and a picture of a smiling snowman were all the old man had ever wrestled up in his store. Sarah and Amanda had devoted heavy amounts of personal cash into transforming O'Mally's into a Christmas wonderland.

"You could be right, love," Amanda said, listening to Bethany reveal her musings on why O'Mally's was constantly full of shoppers. "People do seem to be enjoying the new atmosphere."

Bethany smiled as she watched Amanda gobble down a kosher chili dog. A little chili dripped onto the red and green dress Amanda was wearing.

Sarah, who was sitting at a wooden desk wearing an

identical dress, rolled her eyes. "Want a donut?" she asked Bethany, picking up a holiday-wrapped donut box filled with goodies.

"Oh, I'll take a chocolate snow donut!" Amanda cried out. Before Sarah could move, Amanda snatched out two chocolate donuts covered with white sprinkles. "Hello calories, goodbye waist!"

Bethany let out a giggle. Amanda was nuts. Julie must have read Bethany's thoughts because she giggled, too. "Amanda, are you sure we're related?"

"Afraid so, love," Amanda replied as she inhaled a donut.

Sarah smiled. Oh, how she loved her precious Amanda. "Well, we have work to do, ladies. Julie, if you could tend to the toy aisle, that would be great. Amanda, stay away from the snack café and please try to focus on the arts and crafts aisle. Yesterday, we had a crayon war—it was a disaster. I'll focus on the clothing sections with Amy." She checked the time. "We close at five o'clock today and stay closed until after Christmas. It's going to be a very hectic day." She looked up at Bethany, who was dressed in a green and red dress like everyone else. "Bethany, honey, if you could please help out at the snack café. All the food is fifty percent off, which means the café is going to be overrun and—"

"The entire store is fifty percent off. As soon as we unlock the doors, we're going to be trampled," Amanda pointed out as she inhaled her second donut. "We'll be blessed if we make it to Bethany's coffee shop on time for our Christmas party. I'll leave early to get the pizzas, love. The Snow Falls Pizza Parlor closes at four o'clock today."

Bethany wasn't thinking of Tara at that moment, but as soon as Amanda mentioned the Christmas party, she suddenly remembered the strange young woman. "Oh, I forgot to mention I invited a young lady to our party," Bethany announced quickly. "Her name is Tara Anderson. She's been visiting my coffee shop."

"Anderson..." Sarah put down the box of donuts she was holding and rubbed her bottom lip. "I know of a Curtis Anderson. Mr. Anderson lives alone on Frozen Lake Road, if I'm not mistaken. Also, if I'm not mistaken, he has a daughter who lives in Florida."

Bethany nodded. "Tara is from Florida. West Palm Beach. She's an actress, or so she told me." She sighed. "I believe Tara is lonely. At least, that's how I read the situation. But I must warn everyone, Tara has a sharp mouth on her." She sighed again, thinking of the abrasive young woman. "She can be a bit sarcastic and bitter when she wants to be. If you don't want her attending the Christmas party, I understand. I should have mentioned her to you earlier."

"Well, it is the season to show love, kindness, and mercy," Amanda pointed out cheerily. "Jesus commands us to love everyone, so the more, the merrier, right, girls?"

Julie glanced at Sarah, who shrugged her shoulders. "I suppose you're right, Amanda." Sarah looked up at Bethany. *What are the chances Bethany has been entertaining a dangerous person without knowing it? Edwin McCrandy is behind bars, after all.* "The more, the merrier."

Bethany allowed herself relieved smile. "I can call Tara and ask her to pick up the pizzas for us. I'm sure she'll be glad to do so. Tara is—"

A telephone sitting on the desk cut her off.

"Just a second..." Sarah hurried to answer the call. "O'Mally's...oh, hi, honey...no, Bethany is here with me. Is everything okay? Oh...I see...well, I suppose that is good news in a way...one less monster in the world...okay...I'll tell her...oh...you have to warm up Little Sarah's milk to make her drink it...no, it's okay, sometimes you forget. Okay, bye, honey...love you, too...give Little Sarah a kiss for me."

"What is it?" Bethany asked as soon as Sarah ended the call.

"Well," Sarah drew in a deep breath as she folded her

arms together. "It seems that Edwin McCrandy decided that killing himself was better than going to prison. He was found dead in his jail cell. Hung himself."

"Forgive me if I don't shed any tears." Amanda reached down and got herself a third donut.

Bethany stood silent for a minute, more or less in shock. "Well, that takes care of my fears. I was worried Edwin McCrandy might escape someday and seek revenge. I guess I can sleep a little better now."

"You sure can." Sarah offered a caring smile. "Amanda can leave early and get the pizzas. You can go with her. I'm sure Julie and I can handle things after you leave."

Julie looked into Bethany's eyes, spotting relief pouring out of the woman's eyes. "Merry Christmas," she told her and offered a warm hug. "Now you can have a peaceful time of it."

"I guess so," Bethany agreed, hugging Julie back. She let out a shaky laugh. "This is one Christmas I won't ever forget. Whew..."

Julie took Bethany's hand. "It's almost time to open the stoe. I think a little work might take our minds off our problems."

"I agree," Amanda stated as she munched down her donut. "Let's get to work, ladies. Mama wants a new sweater."

"Silly," Sarah laughed. She picked up a set of store keys and handed them to Amanda. "Go open the doors, honey. I'll be along shortly. I need to call Conrad back and ask him something." She made it seem as if she had to call her husband and ask a marital question.

Amanda, Bethany, and Julie prepared for a long morning and bravely marched out of the warm office.

Sarah quickly called Conrad. "Honey, I need you to do a welfare check, but stay out of sight when you do it..."

Conrad listened to his wife talk as he prepared his sweet

little angel a warm glass of sweet milk. "I'll call Andrew and we'll go see what's going on, Sarah. We'll stay out of sight. I'll call you when I have something, but I have to wait for Mrs. Fleishman to get here before I can leave. It might be a while."

"We have time." Sarah told her husband she loved him and ended the call. "Tara Anderson...I wonder..." She pushed an old desk chair up to a cranky computer and brought up the internet with a quick hand. She began searching for every Tara Anderson in Florida—in West Palm Beach, to be exact. "No Tara Anderson, but there is a Tara Sterling who seems to be a notable name in the theater world." She stared at a photo of a sharp-featured blond-haired girl who seemed to be concealing deep Asian features.

Sarah called Conrad back. "Conrad, can you run a face for me?"

Conrad tensed up. He had neglected to tell Sarah about the call he had received from Detective Habersham. Why? Because it was Christmas and he didn't want to add more worry to anyone, least of all his wife. "Sarah...I think I need to tell you about a call I received." He drew in a deep breath and prepared to have his wife kill him. "Here it goes..."

Sarah listened as Conrad revealed sensitive information concerning a private call he had received. Instead of getting upset, she simply leaned back and began to think. "Can you send me the photo?"

"I'll fax the photo to your office when I get into town. Sarah, I honestly thought the girl left town. I thought we were dealing with a hit-and-run stop. When you called me a few minutes ago...well, a cop can't be right all the time."

"Did you call Andrew?" Sarah asked.

"Not yet. Little Sarah is watching cartoons. I brought her a glass of warm milk and sat with her."

Sarah grew silent for a second. *Either we're dealing with a stupid person or Tara Sterling, assuming she's the person pretending to be Tara Anderson, is very clever. I need to make sure we're dealing with the right person. Tara Sterling is wanted for questioning, not murder, but what are the chances two Taras from West Palm Beach would show up in Snow Falls? I'm sure we're dealing with the same person.* "Conrad, have Andrew do a welfare check on Mr. Anderson. You stay invisible and watch from a distance."

"In other words, spook the chicken and track her every move." Conrad glanced at the back door. A soft snow was falling outside, but the snow was predicted to grow stronger by midnight and turn into a vicious storm. "We have a long day ahead of us."

"Afraid so..." Sarah bit down on her lip. "Conrad, honey, Bethany never told me the name of the woman her dead husband was seeing. Can you find out the name for me? I'm starting to have a bad feeling the last name of that woman might be Sterling."

"I'll have Andrew dig up the name," Conrad promised, then paused. Something in his wife's voice bothered him. "What's eating you, baby?"

"Stupidity," Sarah confessed. "Why would Tara Sterling make it so easy to become a trapped animal? If she's wanted for questioning, why make it so obvious? Also, why keep the name Tara? Why didn't the young woman in question completely change her first name? Why did she tell Bethany she lived in West Palm Beach and that she was an actress? Something isn't adding up, and I fear Bethany is too emotionally worn down to consider the possibility that a new danger might be present. Conrad, you should have seen Bethany's face when I told her Edwin McCrandy was dead...absolute relief."

Conrad looked down at a hard wooden floor. "Looks like Snow Falls might not have a Merry Christmas after all," he said with a sigh. "I have work to do. You stay at the store. I'll drop Little Sarah and Mrs. Fleishman—"

"No, keep Little Sarah at home where she's safe." Sarah

stood up. "Conrad, I think I need to attend a very important Christmas party tonight."

"Sarah—"

"Conrad, honey, Bethany is my friend and she could be in danger. I can't turn my back on her. I know I retired from being a detective, but I can't stop being a detective inside my heart. Please, you have to let me help my friend. Bethany is all alone and she has no one. Didn't we become cops to protect the innocent?"

"I hate it when you make sense and remind me of my oath." Conrad shook his head. "Alright, detective, you're now on duty. Make sure your gun is loaded and ready for action. Shoot first and ask questions later. Aim hard and not easy. Understand?"

"I understand."

"I'll be in touch. Keep your cell phone close, and I love you. Bye." Conrad ended the call with a heavy heart.

"Alright, it's time to clear this town of all the shadows and make sure everyone has a Merry Christmas." Conrad quickly called Andrew. "Get the donut out of your mouth. We have work to do."

Andrew threw his legs off the corner of his desk and grabbed a notepad. "I'm ready..."

As Andrew began writing down a set of instructions, Sarah made another call. "Pete, I was going to call you tomorrow night, you old grouch...yes, I'm calling because I need a favor...police work..."

"Alright, kiddo, tell me what's eating at you and I'll make a few calls," Pete fussed as he chewed on a half-smoked cigar. "I'm supposed to be retired, you know."

"You're sitting in a crummy office eating Chinese food and watching *Bonanza*," Sarah told Pete. "You're waiting for the phone to ring and a new case to arrive because you're bored out of your mind."

"Well, crime is slow right now, so stop jabbering and tell

me what you got, kiddo, before I hang up and go back to fussing at Hoss!" Pete barked.

Sarah smiled. Oh, how she missed Pete. "Tara Sterling...West Palm Beach, Florida...actress...she's wanted for questioning about the murder of a man named Tony Wilthrop. Do some digging on the both of them."

"Will do. Give me a few hours—"

"You have until five o'clock, Pete." Sarah checked the time. "I'll be waiting, and...I love you."

"Don't try to butter me up!" Pete fussed, and then smiled sweetly. "Love you, too, kiddo."

Sarah heard Pete end the call. She leaned back against her office chair and waited for a fax to arrive. "Why would someone lead such an obvious trail of crumbs? It's as if Tara Sterling wanted to be found out, but why?"

As Sarah wondered and waited, Tara Sterling carefully broke through the back door of Bethany's coffee shop, carrying a tank of deadly gas. "Tonight's party is going to be a real...bang," she hissed gleefully to herself, sneaking into a dark kitchen. "After I kill everyone, this coffee shop is going to explode and burn. I'll have my revenge...and I'll die doing it."

What Tara didn't know as she began moving through the dark kitchen was that Sarah was quickly uncovering her very deadly and clever plan of revenge. What Tara also didn't know was that a very sneaky raccoon was watching her.

"Merry Christmas!" Amanda called out cheerily as Tara entered the coffee shop, soaked with snow.

Tara quickly scanned the interior of the coffee shop. Sarah,

Amanda, and Julie were all present. Bethany was in the kitchen preparing to bring out a tray of cookies. "Uh...hi, is Bethany here?" Tara asked, shaking snow off her white coat.

"In the kitchen, love," Amanda beamed as she hummed to Perry Como.

Tara studied her three victims. All three women were dressed in green and red holiday dresses and were wearing red and white stocking caps. Tara fought back a grin. It was going to be fun killing three stupidly dressed women. "My name is Tara. Bethany was expecting me."

Bethany exited the kitchen before anyone could speak. "Cookies...oh, hi, Tara, you're here. Good. Now we can officially begin the party." Bethany hurried out into the front room, carrying a warm tray and Christmas cookies. All the tables in the room had been pushed up against the back wall, forming a buffet-style line. Pizza, cheeseburgers, cakes, pies, and a large punch bowl filled with snow punch sat on the tables. "Everyone, this is Tara, the young lady I told you about this morning."

"Hi, Tara," Julie smiled. "Please, take off your coat. We were just getting ready to play pin the snowball on the snowman."

Tara spotted a poster of a large snowman pinned to the east wall. "Sounds...fun. Uh, I'm a little cold. Mind if I leave my coat on? The heater on my grandfather's truck cut out. It was a miserable drive into town and the snow is really coming down. I'm kind of frozen stiff."

"Sure, you can leave your coat on," Bethany smiled as she set the tray of cookies down onto one of the coffee tables. She shared a quick glance with Sarah, who placed a piece of cheese pizza onto a holiday plate and pretended to focus on the punch bowl.

"Grab some grub and get ready for some fun, love!" Amanda told Tara in a happy voice. "It's just us ladies, so we can have food all over our faces."

"I don't have a problem with that." Julie moved to the tables and began preparing herself a food plate.

"We'll eat and then play pin the snowball on the snowman," Bethany laughed, joining Julie.

Tara watched as all four women began preparing their food plates. She grinned hideously, and then, without any notice, eased a deadly gun out of her front coat pocket. "Eat, ladies," she spoke in a low tone that made everyone turn around and face her, "because it's going to be your last meal."

Bethany spotted Tara raising a vicious gun into the air. Instead of acting shocked, she simply nodded. "So you did kill Tony Wilthrop," she said calmly. "I was praying you were not the Tara Sterling the police are looking for. You managed to change your appearance enough to fool even me. I kept insisting that you were not the Tara Sterling. Well, I was wrong."

Tara grinned. "Your husband and his friends are outside watching," she told Sarah. "I was wondering when you were going to figure out my game. I was actually getting a little worried you weren't going to figure out my game. No matter…I still win, no matter what." Tara focused her deadly eyes on Bethany. "I set the bait. I guess you weren't as smart as I had hoped. I was hoping for a real game of wits."

"Who are you?" Bethany demanded even though she clearly knew the answer.

Tara aimed her gun at Bethany. "I'm the daughter of Donna Sterling. The name ring a bell? Donna was the woman your dear old husband was romancing! Now she's dead—because of you!"

Bethany shook her head. "I didn't kill your mother, young lady."

"Your husband was in a rush to get to his precious attorney because of you! He forced my mother to go with him. My mother was against the entire deal, but your husband kept telling her you were going to destroy him."

Tara narrowed her eyes. "I have a little surprise for everyone. I know the cops are outside watching. Don't worry." She slipped her left hand into her coat pocket and pulled out a black box that had a red glowing switch attached to it. "There is a tank of very explosive gas hooked to a gas line. I hid the tank in the attic and ran a single line to the main gas line. All I have to do is press this little button and...boom! But first, I'm going to kill all of your friends, Bethany. One by one, right in front of you, and will make you suffer. I can tell how much you care about your stupid little friends, so I'm going to take away everyone you care about the same way you took my mother from me!"

"We have to get in there!" Andrew began to move away from the back of a truck.

Conrad grabbed his arm. "Sit tight," he ordered over a howling wind that was pulling a weak, gray sun below the horizon. "We can't move in. It's too dangerous. Sarah is on her own."

"I know the cops are listening," Tara hissed. "If I even suspect the cops are getting close...boom!" She swung her gun over to aim at Sarah. "You cops think you're so smart! I've been watching the entire time. I outsmarted you all."

"Only now you're caught between a rock and a hard place. Why?" Sarah asked, keeping her voice calm. "Why make yourself known?"

"Are you that stupid?" Tara snapped at her. "I plan on dying myself, and joining my mother!" Her eyes began to drip with poisoned lava. "My mother was my everything...and now she's dead! I killed her husband, the man she hated, and bought my time until I found Bethany. Now I'll have my revenge!"

"Sounds to me like you're a very confused and disturbed young lady," Sarah told Tara. "You seem to have created a perfect plan—at least, that's what you believe. But in reality, Tara, your plan is very clumsy, flawed, and reckless...or is it?" Sarah shook her head. "You know your words are being recorded, so you're carrying out a script. The truth is, all you want is money. I did some checking and found out that Tony Wilthrop was your boyfriend. He was the nephew of Richard Wentworth—before you killed him."

"You shut up!" Tara erupted.

"Richard Wentworth worked for Bethany's husband," Sarah continued, ignoring Tara's dangerous outburst. "You used Tony to give you sensitive information, right? You knew your mother was up to no good. Or worse, you knew your mother was going to leave you holding a dangerous drug tab. That's right, Tara—I know you and your mother are in debt to a dangerous drug dealer." She shook her head. "Bethany's husband and your mother died because a drunk driver killed them. That was by accident, no foul play. You wanted your mother to inherit Bethany's husband's money. You two were planning to kill the man...only you were also planning to kill your mother afterward—"

"Shut up!"

"Tony Wilthrop found out about your plan and decided to report you to the police. That's when you killed him—you and Richard Wentworth. Why did Richard Wentworth help you? He became infatuated with you, didn't he? Yes, I think so. But somehow, the police caught on and you were forced to create a new plan of action, right? So you tracked down Bethany and created the plan that's now falling apart right before your eyes. Sound about right?"

Tara began to shake all over. "You shut up or—"

Amanda raised her hand, cutting Tara off. She wasn't

worried about dying, knowing Sarah had the situation under control. "I still don't understand how she was going to force Bethany to turn over money that's sitting in a bank?"

"Bethany?" Sarah turned the floor over to Bethany.

"Do you have the papers, Tara?" Bethany asked. "The legal papers you had my husband's lawyer draw up? After all, Richard Wentworth is helping you, isn't he? At least he was before the FBI swarmed his office today." Bethany looked at Sarah. "Your friend Pete did an amazing job. I can't wait to meet him."

Tara's jaw dropped. "How did you...no, this can't be! I set up everything perfectly. I'm on video at O'Mally's...I made you all believe...now I'm...Richard and I planned everything out...down to the last detail..."

"Your plan is falling apart, isn't it?" Bethany asked. "You planned to fake your death. Richard Wentworth has a new life set out for you all on paper...new birth certificate, social security card, everything...at least he did. Now Richard Wentworth is squealing like a baby. Too bad."

"Okay, time out!" Amanda yelled. "Will someone please tell me how that fruitcake standing over there was going to get Bethany to sign over her money?"

"Pain!" Tara screamed. "Pain can make anyone obey...after Bethany sees me kill you, she'll break! I'll make her suffer! I'll break her! She's weak! I'm in charge! I outsmarted everyone! Do you hear me!" Her sanity began to break down. "I even outsmarted Richard...he's a dead man...do you hear me!"

"Well, Merry Christmas to you, too," Amanda said grumpily. "You sure know how to ruin a good Christmas party. I don't think I'll let you have any pizza."

"Shut up!" Tara aimed her gun at Amanda now. "One more word, and you're dead!"

"Is she?" Sarah asked. "Well, you can kill us, but once the shooting starts, my husband will swarm in here and end your life. And as far as you blowing us all up...well, you can try, but the line connected to the gas tank has been disconnected. Besides, you might want to look over to your right."

"That's right," Bethany added. "Henry, why don't you say hello to Tara."

Tara spun around and spotted Henry aiming his gun at her. "One wrong move and you're dead," he warned. "Put your gun down now, or die. Your choice." His voice clearly told Tara that if she moved one wrong inch, she was a dead woman. "Drop your gun now!"

"Move!" Conrad yelled from outside. "Everyone move in!"

Tara continued to stare at Henry as her body slowly turned into stone. She couldn't move or breathe. "But how...I had it all figured out..."

Before Bethany could say another word, Conrad burst through the front door with his gun at the ready.

"Drop the gun! Drop the gun!" Conrad hollered.

Tara felt her hand turn numb. The gun she was holding simply loosened and began falling like a bag of dead snakes.

Andrew rushed past Conrad and slapped a pair of handcuffs on Tara.

"But how...I had it all figured out...I was in control...you were my scapegoat..."

Bethany put down the plate she was holding and walked to Tara. "Many dark secrets concerning my husband were revealed to me today. Secrets that will help me understand him better. My husband was a very sick man, and so was your mother...and so are you, young lady." Bethany shook her head. "By the way, Richard Wentworth isn't being held by the FBI right now. We bluffed you, but I'm sure in time you will assist the FBI, right? I'm sure you will. You're not the type of person who takes a hard fall alone."

"You...bluffed me?" Tara's eyes grew wide. "You..."

"Young lady, I'm not a stupid woman, and neither is Sarah...or Amanda or Julie...or the cops you see standing before you. That was your mistake. You assumed you could outsmart everyone. You were wrong." She looked at Conrad. "Take her away."

"Henry, take her to the station," Conrad ordered.

"We'll save you some pizza, Henry," Amanda promised. Henry smiled and pulled Tara Sterling out into a hard, cold snow that broke Tara down into a screaming animal.

Conrad approached Sarah. "You're going to give me a nervous breakdown, do you know that?"

Sarah smiled, kissed Conrad, and handed the poor man a slice of pizza. "Eat," she told Conrad, and then moved over to Bethany. "You're not alone," she promised, putting her arm around Bethany. "You have friends."

Bethany looked down at her hands. "Tara had me fooled. If it wasn't for you, Sarah, I...well, maybe I would be dead right now."

"We're only human, love," Amanda told Bethany, putting her arm around the woman's other shoulder. "That little rat had me fooled, too."

"Toss me into the pot and call me silly, too," Julie added, moving close to Bethany.

Bethany looked up at the three women who were shielding her from harm—shielding her with a force field of love no evil could destroy. Tears began to drip from her eyes. "So this is what it's like to have friends—"

"Not friends...sisters, love," Amanda whispered as she tenderly wiped Bethany's tears away.

"Bethany, I know she opened an ugly grave for you, but I pray you can start to heal now that you know the truth about your husband." Sarah placed her head against Bethany's shoulder. "Welcome to Snow Falls, honey."

Bethany closed her eyes and saw Ebenezer Scrooge crawling out of a damp, foggy grave. *I bluffed a killer, and then let a killer nearly bluff me. I'm still hurting...I'm still a little confused...I still feel a little lost...but somehow, I feel everything is going to be alright. Snow Falls is my home now. I have friends who truly care about me...friends I need, and friends who need me. I know the road ahead is going to be tough, but I'm going to be alright. I'll take each day as it comes...take each step one at a time...and pray along the way.*

"Sarah," Bethany finally spoke, "maybe I will write another book. Maybe I'm not such a monster after all. Maybe I'm just a woman who needs to let her heart heal. With that said..." she nodded at the stack of pizza boxes. "Why let all that pizza go to waste? Let's eat."

"I love this gal!" Amanda exclaimed. "Let's eat."

Bethany looked at Julie. "Maybe we can discuss being roommates while we eat, Julie? My cabin has plenty of room."

"Really?" Julie asked, shocked. Bethany nodded. "I would like that very much."

"So would I. And who knows...maybe someday we'll find ourselves two good men and have a full house. In the meantime, let's eat. I'm starving." Rascal scurried out from behind the front counter and joined Bethany. "Now you show yourself," Bethany laughed.

Merry Christmas, Bethany...and welcome to your life in Snow Falls.

Outside, the snow continued to fall.

Far away, in sunny California, a hungry killer threw down Bethany's book and kicked over a cheap lamp. "The perfect murder...don't worry, Bethany, you're going to see the perfect murder. I'll see you soon!" The light attached to the kicked-over lamp flickered and went out, casting darkness onto the face of a nightmare.

"See you real soon, Bethany...real soon."

more from wendy

about wendy meadows

Wendy Meadows is a USA Today bestselling author whose stories showcase women sleuths. To date, she has published dozens of books, which include her popular Sweetfern Harbor series, Sweet Peach Bakery series, and Alaska Cozy series, to name a few. She lives in the "Granite State" with her husband, two sons, two mini pigs and a lovable Labradoodle.

Join Wendy's newsletter to stay up-to-date with new releases. As a subscriber, you'll also get BLACKVINE MANOR, the complete series, for FREE!

Join Wendy's Newsletter Here
wendymeadows.com/cozy

CPSIA information can be obtained
at www.ICGtesting.com
Printed in the USA
LVHW050211080323
741179LV00012B/984

9 798201 949785